AMBUSH ON THE MESA

They needed a regiment, but the Army only sent one man—Hugh Kinzie, Scout. Hugh saddled his dun and rode west. He found the party of men and women ambushed by Red Sleeves, the maniacal Indian chief who hated the white man far more than he feared death. Hugh had only one hope to get them out—his old, battered, still deadly rifle . . .

GORDON D. SHIRREFFS

AMBUSH ON THE MESA

Complete and Unabridged

LINFORD
Leicester

First published in the U.S.A. in 1967 by
Belmont Tower Books,
New York

First Linford Edition
published August 1986

British Library CIP Data

Shirreffs, Gordon D.
   Ambush on the mesa.—Large print ed.—
Linford western library
I. Title
813'.54[F]   PS3569.H56/

ISBN 0-7089-6224-6

Published by
F. A. Thorpe (Publishing) Ltd.
Anstey, Leicestershire
Set by Rowland Phototypesetting Ltd.
Bury St. Edmunds, Suffolk
Printed and bound in Great Britain by
T. J. Press (Padstow) Ltd., Padstow, Cornwall

1

CALL to Quarters blew across the wide parade ground of Fort Craig and died away across the Rio Grande. The New Mexico night was as soft as velvet. Hugh Kinzie led his tired dun across the parade ground towards post headquarters. The dry wind swept the low mesa and flapped the canvas of the long rows of Sibley tents. Yellow lamplight dappled the barren ground from the windows of the post buildings. Hugh tethered his dun, slapped the dust from his clothing and entered head-quarters.

An orderly looked up from his desk as Hugh entered. "Kinzie," he said, "the Old Man has been expecting you."

"I'm here," Hugh said shortly.

The orderly hurried into an inner office and then returned. "Major Roberts will see you, Kinzie. How was it down South?"

"Rough."

Hugh walked into Roberts' office. Major Roberts stood up and held out his hand. He peered at Hugh from under bushy eyebrows. "What's the news from the South?" he asked in his twanging Vermont speech.

Hugh gripped the major's hand and then sat down. "There are Confederates at Fort Thorn. Just a patrol. Baylor has his Second Regiment of Texas Mounted Rifles at Mesilla. General Sibley is *en route* from San Antonio to join Baylor. He is said to have Riley's, Green's and Steel's regiments of mounted rifles; Steele's and Riley's field batteries. Baylor has a few mountain howitzers."

Roberts drummed stubby fingers on his desk. "Then all this talk of the Texans having a big buffalo hunt is strictly nonsense."

Hugh grinned. "They'll be hunting Yankees, sir."

Roberts looked up quickly. "We'll be

ready for them. You've done outstanding work, Hugh. Are you going to stay on as civilian scout?"

"No."

"We need every loyal man for the defence of New Mexico. Why don't you re-enlist? I can get you a sergeant-major's stripes in the Mounted Rifles."

"You know how I feel about that, sir."

Roberts nodded. "Yes. I recommended you for a commission again. The courier brought back the answer from Santa Fe yesterday."

"And?"

Roberts looked away. "There is some question about your loyalty."

Hugh smashed a fist down on his thigh. "Why? Because I was born in Virginia? For God's sake, sir! I left there when I was seven years old to come west to Missouri with my father and mother. I fought for my country in the Mexican War when I was only sixteen. I served honourably in the Mounted Rifles until just last year. I've been scouting for the

Federals since this war started. What more do they want?"

Roberts raised his head. "I wouldn't have recommended you for a commission unless I believed you were loyal."

"How can Colonel Canby turn me down then?"

Roberts shoved a box of cigars towards Hugh. "Take it easy. It just so happens that many of the old regulars have joined the Confederacy."

Hugh took a cigar and angrily bit the end from it. He lit up and drew the smoke gratefully into his lungs. "Officers . . . every one of them. Claiborne, Crittenden, Loring, Lee and Johnston."

Roberts lit a cigar and eyed Hugh through the smoke. "Have you heard from your elder brother Ronald lately?"

Hugh looked up quickly. "No. The last thing I heard he was a captain in the infantry at Fort Buchanan. Why do you ask?"

Roberts leaned forward. "The officer in charge of Fort Buchanan destroyed a large quantity of supplies there when the

4

forts in Arizona were abandoned. The garrison marched to New Mexico."

"Then Ron is here?" asked Hugh eagerly.

"Your brother resigned his commission in the United States Army and went down into Mexico. It is said that he went to Texas and took service with the Confederacy."

Hugh stared at Roberts. "He always believed in state's rights. But he was Virginian to the core. I consider myself as a Missourian."

Roberts waved a hand. "I know. But Ronald Kinzie was disbursing officer at Buchanan. Twenty thousand dollars in negotiable government drafts disappeared at the same time he left for Mexico. Do you understand?"

"That's a damned lie! Ron might have joined the Confederacy—it would be like him—but he'd never steal from the Government!"

Roberts shrugged. "Times and men have changed."

"Do you believe the story?"

"No. Your brother forwarded a letter from Mexico in which he stated he had turned the money over to a certain Lieutenant Winston who was leaving for Fort Ayres. Winston has since vanished."

"Then he has it!"

"Perhaps. You've been to Fort McLane?"

"Near Santa Rita del Cobre? Yes. Major Linde had a battalion of the Second Infantry there up until last June."

"Fort McLane has since been abandoned. But Linde was to have received those drafts from Winston, who was supposed to arrive at Fort McLane with some people from Fort Ayres. Winston never showed up."

"It's rather poor evidence against Ron."

"There is a way you can clear Ron and prove your loyalty, but I hesitate to ask you."

"Shoot!"

"Canby wants those drafts. That's the first part of the problem. The second part is this: Captain Maurice Nettleton commanded Fort Ayres. He was supposed to have left the post some weeks ago, travelling to Fort McLane with his command. Nettleton and his command have vanished. Canby wants a search made for them. I can't send a force to do the job. I need every man I have to defend the Rio Grande Valley should Baylor and Sibley attack us."

"Why is Nettleton so important?"

Roberts leaned forward. "It isn't Nettleton we're interested in as much as it is his wife. Marion Nettleton was Marion Bennett before her marriage. The only child of Shelton Bennett of Missouri."

Hugh whistled softly. "Boss Bennett."

"The very same. Bennett has been raising hell. Orders have been sent to Canby to find her. I don't have to remind you that Shelton Bennett is an important factor in the political picture of Missouri. President Lincoln is anxious to have Missouri held for the Union. If anything happens to Marion Nettleton, Bennett, in his narrow-mindedness, might just throw his influence to the side of the Confederacy."

Hugh grinned wryly. "And you want me to go into Apache country to find twenty thousand dollars and the daughter of a boss politician to prove my loyalty?"

"Not *me*, Hugh. I just thought it might be your chance. Canby is raising unadulterated hell with me for not locating her."

"One man instead of a regiment? Who do you think I am?"

"I don't know of any other man in this department who might possibly do it."

Hugh relit his cigar. "For a posthumous commission? It comes high, particularly when every two-bit politician in New Mexico, not to mention the whole damned United States, is raising a command of his constituents so that they'll vote him in as commanding officer."

"You're a bitter man, Hugh Kinzie."

Hugh studied the officer. "Would you do it?"

"I've been a regular for more years

than I care to admit. Then too, I'm a Vermonter. It makes a difference."

Hugh slapped a hand against his thigh. "If a man is loyal to his country, does it matter *where* he comes from? Winfield Scott is Virginia born."

"So is Robert E. Lee," said Roberts dryly.

Hugh stood up and paced back and forth. "I know in my heart that Ron didn't take those drafts with him. It isn't so much the chance of a commission that drives me on now. It's clearing him."

"Then you'll go?"

"Yes. Tonight. I'll get a fresh horse. I can be in the Black Range Foothills by dawn."

Roberts stood up. "I knew you'd go. I'll need good officers before this war is over. If you succeed, I'll see to it that you get commissioned in my squadron."

Hugh looked down at the faded green stripes along the seams of his trousers. "I'd like that," he said quietly.

"You were one of the best sergeants in

the mounted rifles. Draw anything you need for your trip."

"Can I draw courage?"

"You've a full supply, Hugh."

Hugh gripped Roberts' hand and then left the building. He stood for a time on the parade ground listening to the dry whispering of the desert wind. He looked towards the west, where Dasoda-hae, He That Is Just Sitting There, the giant chief of the Mimbreno Apaches, was king. He was almost in his seventies now, but was still physical and spiritual leader of his tough warriors. The whites knew him by another name . . . Mangus Colorado . . . Red Sleeves.

2

HUGH KINZIE lay in the rustling mesquite looking down at the dim quadrangle of Fort McLane. Someone had played hell there. Roofs had been caved in and the corrals had been torn down. From a busy frontier post it had degenerated into just another ghostly ruin.

Hugh rested on his elbows and studied the terrain. He had reached the hills just before dawn the day before and had stayed hidden all day. At dusk he had gone on, paralleling the old rutted Spanish road which wound through the low hills. A strange feeling had come over him as he travelled. Before the war there had been posts all the way to the Colorado River. Now they had all been abandoned, and the Apaches once again held full sway over their big country. Between Fort Craig on the Rio Grande and Fort Yuma on the Colorado there was nothing to show that the vast lands were still part of the United states. For all he knew he was the only loyal man west of Fort Craig and east of Fort Yuma.

Hugh half-cocked and then capped his Sharps. He eased his Navy Colt from its holster and checked it. Only seven shots between him and hell. But he was at his destination now. He might as well go ahead with his dubious mission.

He passed the post cemetery with its mounded graves and tilted headboards. He stopped beside a tumbledown abode and eyed the littered quadrangle. He padded forward. His boots grated on broken glass and crunched rusting tin cans. Mattresses had been ripped and their contents scattered everywhere. The shattered wood of crates and boxes was mingled with other debris. A pile of Sibley tents and good blankets had been slashed and then set afire.

Hugh walked softly to the old post headquarters. The roof had collapsed. He eyed the mounds of roof beams and dried adobe which filled the interior. It would take him days to dig down into that mess to look for the lost drafts. The wind moaned through the ruins as he completed his inspection. He had known all along that he'd never find them. That left Marion Nettleton to be found in a country where Apaches prowled like tigers of the desert looking for white men . . . and women.

Fort Ayres, as he recalled it, had been a one-company post on a fork of the Gila, about eighty miles to the west. Eighty miles of danger. South of Fort McLane there was nothing except the old Butterfield Trail, now abandoned. Beyond that was almost waterless country clear down to and over the Chihuahua border. North of the abandoned fort was the roughest country he had ever seen. The brooding Black Range, without roads, and with but few known trails. He had heard there were ruins in there built hundreds of years ago by the Hohokam: the Old Ones. They had lived and prospered there, tending their patches of maize, and building their cliff-dwellings, only to vanish many years before the all-conquering whites had invaded the Southwest.

Hugh padded back into the brush. The abandoned fort depressed him. He had to find Marion Nettleton and he had to keep his hide whole. Neither task would be easy, and he knew which of the two was most important to him.

His horse nickered as he approached. He led the buckskin to the north. He missed the speed of his big dun but the buckskin had a stamina in him that the dun lacked.

There was a water-hole in the Pinos Altos some miles north of the abandoned fort. He followed the rutted track through the darkness until the buckskin whinnied. He had smelled the water. Hugh picketed the horse and went ahead on foot. He halted a hundred yards from the water-hole and tested the night with his senses. There seemed to be nothing but the night wind rustling the brush, but still he waited. It was a sixth sense he had developed in his years on the frontier. He circled the water-hole and dropped flat on a knoll which overlooked the low ground around the water-hole. Apaches would always avoid camping near water-holes. They camped on high ground, water or no water.

He eyed the brush about the water-hole. Something moved. Then a burro brayed softly. Hugh moved downwind and crept through the brush until he could see the dull sheen of the water. A man was sitting up in his blankets. Hugh could see the dim silhouette of his steeple-crowned hat. Probably a Mex.

The man stood up and raised a rifle. "Who is there?" he called out in Spanish.

"A friend."

The rifle hammer clicked back. "Who are you?" called out the man.

Hugh took a chance. "An army scout."

"There are no American troops this far west of the Rio Grande."

"I am."

"Come forward then with your hands high."

Hugh snapped his carbine ring to the swivel on his sling, then swung the Sharps behind his back. He eased his Colt in its holster, then walked forward out of the brush.

The Mexican was a little man. He eyed Hugh. "What do you do here?"

"I am looking for a party of Americans."

"I am alone here."

Hugh looked about. The burro was picketed in the brush. There was no one else in sight. "I want water," he said.

"There is enough for you."

"Then I'll get my horse."

The Mexican hesitated. He scanned the swaying brush.

"Why are you afraid? Do I look like an Apache?"

"There are none within miles. I made sure of that, señor."

"Then let me get my horse."

"I will be right behind you."

Hugh shrugged. He walked back towards the buckskin with the little Mexican a safe distance behind him.

Hugh led the horse to the water and let him drink. He turned to the little man. "I am Hugh Kinzie," he said.

"Jorge Dura, at your service."

"What do you do here, Jorge?"

Dura lowered his rifle. "When the soldiers left the fort they did not take some of their horses. They are in these hills. I am looking for them."

Hugh knelt and drank. The edge of the waterhole was dotted with hoof marks into which the water had seeped. There had been many horses there, and not too long before. "You have seen Americans hereabouts?" he asked over his shoulder.

Dura nodded. "Some Americans were west of here. They were soldiers."

"Any women?"

"Yes . . . two of them."

Hugh stood up and held out his tobacco pouch. Dura cradled his rifle on his left arm and took the pouch. He swiftly rolled a cigarette. "This is dangerous country for Americans," he said.

"I know."

Dura lit up. His eyes were hard in his

small brown face. "Why do you look for them?"

"I have been ordered to do so."

Dura sucked at his cigarette. "They had good horses and weapons. Pack mules, laden with supplies."

"Which way did they go?"

Dura jerked a thumb over his shoulder. "Into the Pinos Altos. Towards the head-waters of the Gila."

Hugh looked at the dark heights. "Why?" he asked, almost to himself.

Dura rested his rifle butt on the ground and leaned on the long barrel. "I do not know. There is no way out of those mountains. Perhaps they went there to avoid the Mimbrenos."

Hugh nodded. Whoever was in charge of the party didn't know that country. Few white men had been in there. It was an unmapped wilderness. Beyond the mountains were the Plains of San Augustin. If they got through they could turn east towards the Rio Grande. "*If* they got through," he said aloud.

Dura shrugged. "It is madness."

Hugh led the buckskin from the water. Dura bothered him. No man who knew Apaches and feared them would camp near a water-hole at night.

"Where do you go?" asked Dura.

"Back to the Rio Grande."

Dura glanced down at his rifle. "That is a fine horse you have."

Hugh nodded. He rested his hand on his pistol butt. "I intend to keep him."

Dura smiled. He knew these big Americanos and the skill they had with the revolving pistols. "Yes," he said quietly. "Go with God, friend."

"Go with God, Jorge Dura."

Hugh led the buckskin around the water-hole, Dura watched him. Then he saddled his burro and packed his blankets. He mounted and rode swiftly to the south. Mangus Colorado would welcome news of a party of rich Americans wandering around in the rough hills. Perhaps Jorge Dura could get his hands on some of their riches, through the graciousness of Mangus Colorado. It was well worth the risk.

3

THE false dawn was greying the eastern sky when Hugh found the first traces of the party ahead of him. A spur lay in the rough trail. A mile beyond that he found many tracks on a soft patch of earth. They were damned careless about covering their route. An Apache kid could have trailed them without half trying.

The sun was up when he found another trace of them. A horse had fallen on a rough patch of the trail. Boot tracks showed where they had stood around the fallen horse and got him up on his hooves. It was as plain as a page of print.

The hills crowded in on Hugh as he went on. There was no chance of losing the trail, for there was no other route for them to follow. From the tracks he deduced that there were at least a dozen people in the party.

He looked back to the south as he climbed a ridge. A thread of smoke showed against the sky like coarse hair lying on pale blue cloth. He rubbed his bristly jaw. Farther to the west another scarf of smoke hung against the sky. Now he knew there was no chance of going back to the south.

He crossed a shallow rushing stream, probably a fork of the Gila. They had watered their horses here. The tracks showed plainly on the far side of the stream. He followed the great valley, constantly looking back over his shoulder. The smoke had drifted away.

Cholla, agave and some mescal stippled the valley floor, while above him the slopes were clothed with juniper, piñon and scrub oaks. He looked up ahead. The mountains were high, rough and seemingly endless. It looked like a one-way trip into uncharted country.

High and higher he went. Douglas firs, ponderosa pines and spruces began to appear. A deer surveyed him from a slope, then disappeared into the trees.

Long-crested jays chattered at the lone rider who disturbed their secluded haunts. A black bear shambled off in the distance. But there was no sign of human life other than the imprint of hooves, always going north.

He was almost certain that he was on the trail of the Nettleton party, for he couldn't figure out who else it could be. If they had been Confederate sympathizers they would have trended southward. They were making a trail through that wilderness as though they were travelling on a highway back in civilized country. Hugh was almost tempted to turn back and make for the Rio Grande, but there was always the memory of those smoke signals against the vast sky behind him.

A massive peak towered at least eight thousand feet high to his left. Far to the north he could see another giant of the mountains. It was a country he could have enjoyed if the tigers of the human species weren't somewhere behind him. No matter how careful he was about his own trail, the trail of the party he was following was too plain to erase. Still, one man might get into the mountains and get away from any pursuers. The temptation was strong.

The stream was wider now. He reached a place where it forked. Beyond the fork he could see land which had once been cultivated. Nature had almost erased the signs.

Darkness mantled the mountains, and he was just about to seek a hiding place for the night when he caught the odour of burning wood borne to him on the gentle wind.

Hugh dismounted and took his carbine. He led the buckskin into a thicket and tethered it. Then he went forward through the trees towards the smell of the smoke.

He could see the flickering of flames as he topped a rise. He squatted low and eyed the fire. The murmuring of voices came to him. Americans. The odour of cooking meat mingled with the smell of the smoke. Beyond the fire he could see horses. A soldier stood guard on a knoll, leaning on his rifle, but he was watching the people at the fire rather than the darkness behind him. Having a guard there really didn't make any difference, for the Mimbrenos could have ringed that camp silently as ghosts, waiting for their chance to move in.

Hugh stood up and walked forward. "Hello, the camp!" he called. Then he prudently stepped behind a tree. The guard whirled and raised his rifle. The rest of the people stood about the fire, staring into the darkness. A woman walked into the shadows. A tall officer swiftly drew out his pistol.

"Who is it?" called out the guard.

"Hugh Kinzie. Scout from Fort Craig."

"Come forward into the light!"

"Put out that damned fire, you fools! Are you trying to make sitting ducks out of yourselves?"

"Who does he think he is?" snapped an officer.

Hugh came forward, holding his carbine above his head. A slightly plump officer with captain's bars on his shoulder straps stepped forward. "Captain Maurice Nettleton," he said. "We're from Fort Ayres. Who sent you?"

Hugh grounded his carbine and rested his hands on it. "Major Benjamin Roberts, commanding Fort Craig."

Nettleton tugged at his dark side whiskers. "How did you find us?"

Hugh looked at the blazing fire. "It wasn't hard," he said dryly. "You've left a trail plain enough for an *ish-ke-ne* to follow."

The tall officer came forward. He was only a few inches taller than Hugh but was half again as wide. His shoulders filled out his blouse, threatening to break through the seam. "*Ish-ke-ne?* Say, who the hell are you?"

Hugh ignored the big man. "Tell your men to douse that fire," he said to Nettleton.

"But we haven't eaten yet," said Nettleton.

Hugh walked forward. He kicked dirt

over the fire. "You'll be eating in hell by dawn if you don't put it out."

The tall officer placed his hand on the butt of his pistol and swaggered forward. "I'd like proof of who you are," he said threateningly.

Hugh looked into the face of the officer. His eyes were the coldest grey-green he had ever seen. "I told you who I was," he said quietly.

"I know that. What proof do we have you're Hugh Kinzie from Fort Craig?"

A woman came out of the darkness. "It's Hugh Kinzie, all right," she said quietly. "Hello, Hugh."

Hugh turned. "Katy Corse," he said.

Katy Corse brushed back her dark hair. "It's like you to show up in the wilderness," she said quietly. "And like you to vanish just as quickly."

Hugh flushed. "What are you doing here, Katy?"

The big officer gripped Hugh by the shoulder. "I was talking to you," he said. "Don't you know an officer when you see one?"

Hugh looked the big man up and down. "Yes. Why?"

Nettleton came forward. "Now, Mr. Clymer," he said quickly. "I want no trouble."

Hugh looked about the camp. There were eight other men watching him. One of them was an officer. The others were enlisted men, with the exception of a gaunt man who was dressed in sombre black. "Where were you planning to go, Captain Nettleton?" he asked.

Nettleton wet his lips. "We tried for the Rio Grande and heard the Mimbrenos were between us and the river. We didn't want to go too far south because of the Confederates. So we decided to come north through the mountains, then turn east towards the Rio Grande near Soccorro."

"Just like that," said Hugh dryly. "Who knows the way through that?" He waved a hand towards the black bulk of the mountains.

Nettleton flushed. "There was nothing else we could do."

Hugh kicked more dirt on the fire. He looked at the closest enlisted man. "Get some water," he said.

The enlisted man got a big canteen and emptied it on the burning wood.

Hugh stood there in the dimness. The pungent odour of the wet wood floated about him. "There's no more time to talk," he said. "Let's get moving."

Clymer raised his head. "You're just an enlisted man," he said. "You've got all-fired guts taking charge."

Hugh shook his head. "I'm a civilian scout, Clymer. It's obvious there isn't a man here who knows the Apaches and this country. If you want to get out of these damned mountains with a whole skin you'll do as I say."

Clymer raised a thick hand. Nettleton drew himself up. "See to it that the horses are ready, Mr. Clymer," he said.

Clymer eyed the captain for a moment, then spat deliberately into the smoking embers. "Phillips!" he roared.

The third officer came forward through the drifting smoke. Clymer thrust out a thick arm. "Get the horses ready," he said.

Hugh rubbed his jaw. "Is your wife here, sir?" he asked Nettleton.

Clymer whirled. "What's it to you?" he snapped.

"Is she here, sir?" asked Hugh quietly.

Nettleton nodded. "Of course she is. She's resting in her tent. Why do you ask?"

"Her father has been riding hell out of the War Department to find her. That's all."

Nettleton plucked at his lower lip. "I was worried about that."

Clymer waved a hand. "I could have got her through safely," he said loudly.

Nettleton watched the big officer walk away. "What do you want us to do, Kinzie?" he asked.

"Move north to find a place where we can defend ourselves."

"You fear an Apache attack?"

"Yes."

Nettleton swallowed. He looked off

into the darkness. "I'll get my wife," he said. He hurried off.

Katy Corse looked at Hugh. "It's been quite a while, Hugh," she said.

Hugh nodded. "Where's your husband?" he asked.

"I didn't get married," she said quietly.

"So?"

"Herbert died a month after you left Fort Buchanan."

The enlisted men were saddling the horses. A mule brayed. "Damn you, jughead," said a trooper. "You got the biggest mouth."

Katy Corse looked at Hugh and then turned on a heel. She walked towards the tent amongst the trees.

A man wearing corporal's stripes looked after Katy. "A nice girl," he said.

"Yes," said Hugh softly. "I never expected to see her again."

"She came through the Gila country a week or so before we left Fort Ayres. Said she was heading for the Rio Grande. There was no way for her to go on. Captain Nettleton made her wait until we were ready to leave. I'm Harry Roswell. I've heard of you, Kinzie. You used to be a sergeant in A Company of the Mounted Rifles."

"Yes." Hugh impatiently looked at the men working amongst the horses and mules. "They act like they've got all thumbs."

Roswell nodded. "We're a mixed-up lot here, Kinzie."

"Three officers and a handful of enlisted men. Where are the rest of the men from Fort Ayres?"

"We had a beef herd at the post. Nettleton was scared to death he'd get blamed if we lost them. He started the herd out under charge of Mr. Winston and most of the men."

"So?"

"Chiricahuas stampeded the herd right through their first night's bivouac. We found what was left of some of them the next day. It wasn't pretty. Nettleton lost his nerve and headed into the hills. Short of supplies and low on ammunition. That's us."

"What's on those pack mules?"

Roswell laughed dryly. "Mrs. Nettleton's clothes. Nettleton's silver service and dress uniforms. Records from Fort Ayres."

"That all?"

"Yes. Wait . . . I forgot . . . There are some cases of liqueurs and brandy."

"Nettleton's?"

"Nettleton's."

"For God's sake!"

"Do not take the name of the Lord thy God in vain," a sepulchral voice said just behind Hugh.

"Who are you?" asked Hugh as he turned.

"Do not blaspheme. I am Isaiah Morton."

Morton was the gaunt-looking civilian Hugh had seen in the background. Even in the dimness he could feel the burning eyes of the man studying him.

Roswell spat. "Morton joined us on the trail west of Fort McLane. Said he was going to convert Mangus Colorado."

"They are God's children, even as you and I, Brother Roswell."

Roswell snorted. "That's open to argument."

"Roswell! Where the hell are you?" The harsh voice sounded like a stick being dragged along a picket fence.

Roswell grinned. "That's the first soldier," he said. "I'd better get busy."

A thick-bodied man came up in the darkness. The stripes and diamond of a first sergeant showed on his sleeves.

"Hello, Matt," said Hugh easily.

Matt Hastings thrust his head close to Hugh. "Kinzie! I thought you had taken a discharge."

"I did."

Hastings raised his head. "You're a scout now?"

"Yes."

"The army must be hard up for good scouts."

Hugh tilted his head to one side. "*And* first sergeants. So you finally got your diamond, Matt. You bucked hard enough for it."

Hastings looked back over his shoulder. "I know more about soldiering than any man jack in this J Company outfit."

Hugh nodded. Matt Hastings hadn't changed. Hugh had known him at Fort Stanton and later in Arizona. He was a ring-tailed roarer, self-educated, with the biggest bump of self-esteem on any horse soldier Hugh had ever met in his years of service.

"Well, don't I?" snapped Hastings.

"You sure as hell have forgotten anything you learned about Apaches. Camping in front of a fire."

"There aren't any Apaches within fifty miles."

"Too bad you didn't look back over your shoulder some time this afternoon. You would have seen their signal smokes."

"Boots and Saddles!" roared Clymer through the darkness.

Hugh went back for his buckskin and stood there for a time listening to the night sounds. It was no use. There was enough uproar from the darkened camp to drown out anything else he might have heard.

There was a slender woman standing beside Maurice Nettleton when Hugh came back to the camp. She wore a scarf over her dark hair. Nettleton helped her up on a horse. Hugh looked curiously at her as he mounted. Her face was in shadow, but he could see that she was pretty. He wondered if Boss Bennett would ever see her again.

The noisy cavalcade rode up the trail. Hugh dropped back to cover the rear. Isaiah Morton jogged along on his sway-backed nag. The jackleg preacher looked up at the dark heights looming ahead of them. "A land of darkness, as darkness itself; and of the shadow of death, without any order, and where the light is as darkness," he said dolefully.

Hugh glanced at him. "Have you got a gun?" he asked.

"No."

Hugh leaned over and slashed his reins across the rump of the preacher's nag.

"Then get up there and do your prophesying!"

A trooper was sitting his horse at the side of the trail. He grinned at Hugh. "I can't prophesy, scout," he said. "But I can shoot."

"Good!"

"The name is Chandler Willis."

"Hugh Kinzie."

Willis swung his carbine across his thighs. He shifted his chew and spat. "Looks like a long night," he said laconically.

"Yes. What kind of officers do you have here?"

"Nettleton lives by the book. Never goes far without looking for some regulation to cover what he's doing. Ain't never quite sure of himself for my money."

"And Clymer?"

Willis grinned. "Fancies himself a real stud with the ladies. Got the morals of an alley cat. Lets Nettleton think he's runnin' the shebang. Darrell Phillips ain't a bad hombre. Got breedin', he has.

Might make a good soldier if he didn't have to serve under those other two."

"What kind of an officer was Lieutenant Winston?"

"One of the best. A real man. Wasn't with us long. Come from Fort Buchanan on special duty, or so I heard tell."

"What kind of special duty?"

Willis eyed Hugh. "How should I know?" All I know, is that Nettleton wouldn't send Phillips out with them steers, and Clymer wouldn't go. So Nettleton orders Winston. He *had* to go."

Hugh nodded. "Did they find Winston's body?"

"Yep. Only way we could tell him was by his uniform."

Hugh looked west. Maybe the drafts had been trampled into the dirt along with the bodies of the troopers. Maybe the Apaches had found them and thrown them away, not knowing their value. There wasn't a chance now of clearing Ron. He shrugged, then looked up the column. He could see Katy Corse riding beside Marion Nettleton. Now and then she steadied the captain's wife in the saddle when they hit rough spots on the trail. Hugh wondered if he could finish the second part of his task. Chances looked slim on that too.

Hugh looked back down the dim trail. Below them he could see an eye of fire winking in the darkness. The wind had fanned an ember into life. These greenhorns had left a trail as easy to follow as the Oregon Trail across the plains of Kansas.

Willis looked back. "You think them 'Paches are back there somewheres?"

"I know it, Willis."

They went on through the darkness with fear riding close behind them.

4

CAPTAIN NETTLETON called a halt just when the false dawn showed over the eastern heights. Hugh spurred forward, leaving Chandler Willis as rear guard. Nettleton was close beside his wife, holding her in her saddle. "We'll stop here and make a fire," he said to Hugh.

"No fires," said Hugh shortly.

Able Clymer stood up in his stirrups. "Captain Nettleton is in command, Kinzie."

Hugh looked at the belligerent bull moose of a man. "We'll have cold tack," he said quietly.

Darrell Phillips rode forward and then turned his horse. "There's some kind of an old wall here," he said. "It might serve as a defensive position."

Clymer spat. "Listen to the soldier," he said.

Hugh kneed his buckskin past Clymer. He rode up to Phillips. Someone, long ago, had built a wall in front of a steep slope of rock. "It'll do," said Hugh.

Clymer was arguing with Nettleton about something. His voice was too low for Hugh to hear what he was saying.

Nettleton straightened himself in his saddle. "We'll do as the scout says, Mr. Clymer. We must trust him."

Darrell Phillips' handsome face darkened. "Clymer is a bully," he said.

Hugh nodded. "He's still obeying orders though."

Phillips nodded. "Yes, but for how long? If he had his way we'd all be under his filthy thumb." He looked at Marion Nettleton. "She's exhausted," he said.

"Katy is holding up."

"There's a difference. Marion is gentle bred."

"Out in this country a woman is judged for what she can do rather than how she was bred."

Phillips' dark eyes studied Hugh. "You knew her before?"

"Yes. Last year when I was at Fort Buchanan."

"Good friends, I take it?"

Hugh looked quickly at the officer. "Yes. She was engaged to Herbert Oglesby, a corporal in the dragoons."

"I see. She'd make a good wife for an enlisted man."

Hugh leaned forward. "She'd make a good wife for *any* man, Mr. Phillips." He spurred his buckskin back towards the party.

Phillips shrugged. He looked at Katy Corse. She was riding astride, like a man. Her shapely legs were exposed from the knees down, and she seemed to be perfectly at home in the saddle. For the first time since he had seen her at Fort Ayres he realized that she was a damned attractive woman.

Hugh sat his buckskin as the enlisted men carried food and weapons behind the low wall. Marion Nettleton was seated on a rock. Her husband bustled about her, pulling her shawl about her shapely shoulders. Hugh eyed her. Her oval face

41

had evidently been protected against the hot suns of the South-west, for it still had a cameo quality to it. Her eyes were large, almost too large for her face. There was a petulant look about her full lips.

"Are you all right, my dear?" asked Nettleton.

"Maurice, do stop annoying me," she said. "I'll have my coffee here."

Nettleton looked up at Hugh and then bit his lip. "We're not to have a fire," he said.

"Why? I want hot coffee. It's such a little thing to ask."

Nettleton looked at Hugh. Hugh shook his head. He kneed his horse down the trail. Behind him he heard her petulant voice. "I'd like to know who is in command here, Maurice."

Willis was squatted on a rock above the trail. "No signs yet," he said.

"There will be."

Willis looked up the canyon. "What's up there?"

"Damned if I know."

The trooper shifted his chew. "Hell! What a mess!"

"I'll go along with you on that."

"A man or two could get through, travelling at night, lying low by day."

Hugh studied the enlisted man. "I think so. But we have two women to take care of."

"Who? Me? I didn't enlist to take care of no women."

"You're still under orders, Willis."

"Yeah. But for how long? Clymer hates Nettleton's guts. Phillips hates Clymer's guts. Sergeant Hastings hates everybody's guts."

"And you?"

The cold pale eyes held Hugh's. "I'm thinking about my guts."

Hugh looked down at his Sharps. "You'll stick," he said.

Willis shifted a little. "Mebbe. Mebbe not. Don't threaten me, Kinzie. I don't scare easy. Besides, there's others in this outfit as ain't too happy about herding these officers and women through this hell-hole of a country. You'll find out in time."

Hugh rode back down the trail. He was a good two miles from the temporary camp when he saw the smoke drifting from a peak. It was closer than it had been yesterday. He rolled a smoke and hooked his left leg about his saddlehorn. He lit up and eyed the distant smoke. The horses were worn thin. They needed at least a day's rest. There was a hell of a trail ahead of them.

Hugh rode back to the camp just as the sun showed up over the eastern heights. The women were resting on blankets. Isaiah Morton was reading a battered Bible. Corporal Roswell was up the slope with his carbine resting across his thighs. A burly private stepped in front of Hugh. "I'm Dan Pearce," he said in a New York accent. "What's the odds of us getting through, scout?"

Hugh slid from his saddle. "Fair."

Pearce had a hard face with small green eyes. There was a furtive look about him. "You talk with Willis?" he asked.

"About what?"

"Breaking loose to try for the Rio Grande."

"Yes."

"So?"

"If he goes, he goes alone. If I see him taking off, I'll kill him."

Pearce raised his head. "Hardcase, eh?"

"No. But I've got a job to do and I aim to do it."

Hugh turned his back on Pearce. Pearce stared at Hugh's broad back for a moment, then he walked down the trail towards Willis. The two of them sat on the rock ledge, talking quietly.

A trooper was busy picketing the horses. Hugh walked over to him. "Put them on separate picket lines," he said.

The trooper turned a good-humoured face towards Hugh. "Can I ask why?"

"If they're stampeded we can save most of them. On one picket line the whole kit and caboodle would go."

The trooper nodded. "By God, I'da

never thought of that. The name is Jonas Stevens."

Hugh nodded. "You're not getting much help," he said. He uncoiled a picket line and drove the picket deep into the soft soil. He picketed Phillips' fine chestnut.

Stevens looked back at the camp. "Don't seem to be any of them who want to work together. When I enlisted at Jefferson Barracks in fifty-nine we got lectures on how the army always works as a team. Looks like I'm the only one around here that remembers it."

Hugh picketed another horse. "I do," he said quietly.

They worked together picketing the horses near a patch of grass. Hugh walked over to the pack mules. They were dead beat, for no one had thought of removing their packs. Stevens helped him remove the packs. "Poor jugheads," he said.

Abel Clymer came towards them. "Take it easy with those packs," he said.

Hugh turned and shoved one of them at the big officer. Clymer staggered back until he got his balance. "Damn you!" he said.

Hugh grinned. "Pitch in," he said.

Clymer threw the pack on the ground at Hugh's feet. For a moment he eyed him angrily, then he turned on a heel and strode towards his own horse. He took the saddlebags from it and placed them over his arm. He looked back at Hugh and then strode to the camp.

"Nice fella," said Stevens dryly.

"Bull moose."

"Yeah, but he ain't no push-over, Kinzie. Watch yourself."

"Were you there when Winston and his men were found?"

Stevens shuddered. "Yes. What a mess!"

"Any of Winston's personal baggage found?"

"None. Everything was stamped into the ground. Men, blankets, food . . . everything. Why do you ask?"

"I thought someone might have brought his effects along. For his family, you know."

"Nope. Nothing. Besides, we got enough of a load with Nettleton's personal property. Silver, liquor, clothing and such like. Practically no food, but all of Nettleton's stuff. Hell of a note, ain't it?"

Hugh nodded. He picketed a mule. Stevens studied him as he worked. He rubbed his bristly jaw and then shrugged. "*Personal* effects," he said dryly.

Hugh walked back to the camp.

A neat little soldier holding a tin plate came towards Hugh. He held it out. "Embalmed beef and hardtack," he said quietly. "It isn't much, I'll allow, but just about all we have."

Hugh waved a hand. "Keep it. I've got my own supplies."

The little man nodded. "Thanks. I'm Myron Greer, orderly for the officers."

"Nice job," said Hugh.

Greer shrugged. "I was company clerk at Ayres. Mr. Clymer told me to take over as orderly to relieve Willis. He said Willis was a man, not a frightened worm."

Greer spoke in cultured tones. The man had been educated. He didn't look like the type who would make a hard-riding, hell-for-leather dragoon.

Hugh rolled a smoke. "How is it an educated man like yourself ended up as a company clerk in the dragoons, Greer?"

Greer smiled sadly. "Liquor."

"I've heard that one before. My old squadron commander used to say that when he got a clerk worth anything the man was a drunkard."

Greer looked up. "Kinzie, if it weren't for whisky there wouldn't be any clerks in the army. You wouldn't happen to have a drink, would you?"

Hugh shook his head. There was a bottle of mezcal in one of his saddlebags, but he knew damned well Greer wouldn't settle for one drink. He'd need the whole bottle.

Nettleton came over to them. "Greer!" he said pettishly. "Mrs. Nettleton wants some cold clear water."

Greer held out his free hand. "The canteens are full, sir."

"Find a spring."

"Yes, sir."

Hugh shook his head. "He'll have to stay here."

"Afraid he'll run off?" snapped Nettleton. "Greer? He's scared to death right now."

Hugh looked south. There was still a wisp of smoke against the sky. "So am I," he said.

Greer shambled off towards the camp. Nettleton took out a silver cigar case, selected a cigar, clipped the end with a silver clipper which depended from a silver chain. He put the cigar into his mouth and lit it. "What do you suggest we do?" he asked.

"Rest here. I doubt if they can get past us to attack from the west, east or north. Willis is on guard. I'm going to scout up the canyon."

"There are no Apaches there."

"We don't know the country. From now on we'll have to find a trail. It'd be too damned easy to end up in a box canyon and have to backtrack. We'd lose hours, if not days."

"I see. What do you think our chances are?"

Hugh took out his tobacco pouch. "You're the third or fourth person who has asked me that today."

Nettleton jerked his cigar from his mouth. "I don't want you talking too much to these enlisted men. Keep your counsel for the officers."

Hugh rolled a smoke. "The enlisted men are in this too," he said quietly.

Nettleton's face tightened. He looked down at the green-striped trousers Hugh wore tucked into his boots. "You were an enlisted man yourself?"

"Yes."

"Mounted Rifles?"

Hugh nodded as he lit up.

"They never did have much respect for an officer."

Hugh looked at the angry officer. "I didn't find it so. I do recall one of our surgeons saying that the officers of the Mounted Rifles were all gentlemen, brave and generous to a fault—but the most cantankerous lot he had ever met. There

51

wasn't much chance for an enlisted man to be disrespectful to an officer in *my* regiment, Captain Nettleton."

Nettleton looked away. "Well, get on with your job." He strode back towards the camp.

Hugh walked to his horse and got his canteen and Sharps. Katy Corse came up and placed her hand on the buckskin's nose. "You're not taking him, are you?" she asked.

"No."

"I didn't think you would. He's tired."

"He got more bottom in him than any other mount here."

"I believe it."

Katy brushed back her dark hair. "You've never forgiven me, have you, Hugh?"

"You made your choice."

"You never gave me much hope."

"I didn't fall all over you like Herbert Oglesby did."

"Herbert was a fine man."

Hugh hooked his canteen to his belt. "You would have ended up being a corporal's wife, perhaps a sergeant's wife, Katy."

"So? You were just a sergeant."

"I'll get my commission."

She leaned against the horse. "*If* we get out of here."

"We've got to."

She studied him. "I used to think you were different from your brother, but now I think differently."

"How so?"

"He was all business. Is it true he joined the Confederates?"

"That's what they're saying."

"And you?"

He looked up quickly. "You know I'll stay with the Union."

"This war will split a lot of families."

"Ron and I were never very close."

"Maybe that's why you want a commission, to prove to yourself you're as good a man as he is."

"Katy, sometimes you talk too much."

She smiled. "You haven't changed."

"I'm too old to change, Katy." He unsaddled the buckskin and dropped the saddle on the ground. "Did you know Lieutenant Winston?"

"Yes. I rode with him from Fort Buchanan to Fort Ayres. He practically ordered me to."

"I can't imagine anyone giving *you* orders," he said dryly.

"Why do you ask about him?"

"Just curious."

She shook her head. "There's more to it than that. It's about those government drafts, isn't it?"

"Yes."

She looked towards the camp. "I think he had them with him. They were part of your brother's responsibility, weren't they?"

Hugh nodded.

"I stayed at Fort Ayres when he went on with the beef cattle. He was sent to his death. The cattle weren't worth the loss of all those men and especially of a man like him."

"What about the drafts?"

"I'm not sure he had them, Hugh, but he was always so careful to sleep with his head on his saddlebags. He protested against having to take charge of the beef herd but Nettleton insisted. Nettleton really wanted Abel Clymer to lead the herd—just to get rid of him—but Clymer has Nettleton under his control. At least he did until you got here."

"So?"

"When we reached the place where the cattle had been stampeded, Mrs. Nettleton and I were ordered to stay back so that we wouldn't see what had happened. From what the men tell me, it was awful. But no drafts were brought back to the camp. I'm almost sure of that."

"Who led the men to the place where Winston was killed?"

"All three of the officers went."

"Anyone else?"

"Corporal Roswell, Privates Pearce, Willis and Stevens." She gazed at him closely. "What are you thinking about, Hugh?"

"About going on a scout."

"Is that all?"

"That's all," he said shortly. He walked away from her.

As Hugh passed the camp he heard Mrs. Nettleton call out. "Katy! Do get some water and bathe my temples, like a good girl."

Hugh looked back as he reached the trees. Mrs. Nettleton acted as though everyone in the camp were enlisted in her personal service. There was one person who wasn't—Hugh Kinzie.

5

THE trail didn't improve as Hugh walked north from the camp. It was tough going afoot, even for a man in top physical condition. Deer eyed him from afar, seemingly unafraid of him, and he knew by that sign that they were unaccustomed to seeing humans in their country. As he went on, he occasionally saw ancient fields which had been cultivated by the Hohokam.

It was about noon when he found the trail. It was plainly marked on the earth, trending to the north-west into a rough-walled canyon. There were no indications of wheel ruts nor hoof marks. It had been made by foot travellers, and had been well used.

Hugh shoved back his hat and wiped the sweat from his forehead. He eyed the trail, following it until it was lost to sight in thickets and rock formations, beyond which he could see a humped shape rising high into the sky—a rocky mesa stippled with scrub trees and big pines. He wondered who had made that trail and where it went. He looked to the north-east. There the country was a jumbled mass of mountains, seemingly impassable. Maybe the trail led to the San Francisco, for its headwaters were to the north-west. To follow the trail would entail hard marches, forcing the party to go miles out of their way. But possibly there was a way to trend east again towards the Rio Grande. Yet he did not want to chance breaking a way through the range to the east.

Hugh sipped water from his canteen and then began to follow the trail. There were places where rock slides covered it. There were other places where floods had swept away all traces of the trail, like a giant broom. But he found it again after he had lost it for a time. The walls of the canyon came close together and he walked along looking high above him to see brush and greying driftwood wedged in cracks and crannies. A flash flood would fill the narrow canyon with water many feet deep, sweeping everything before it.

Long shadows were slanting down the slopes when he climbed over a jumbled mass of rock thickly grown with thorny brush. Beyond him he could see where the canyon widened; its walls slanted back on the left below the great mesa he had seen. To the right the walls were almost sheer, seemingly awaiting a gun shot to make them crumble in an avalanche. He looked up the canyon, but the shadows were thick up there and a great shoulder of rock protruded into the canyon to block his vision. There was no way of knowing whether or not the trail continued around the rock shoulder or petered out in a chaos of rock.

He sat on a rock and studied the canyon. There was a curious, even line of rock, high on the left wall. It rose in several tiers and seemed to be of a different colour than the rest of the rock. Dark patches, curiously even, showed at regular intervals along the rock line. He felt for his field glasses and then remembered he had left them at the camp.

He stood up and picked up his carbine, still looking at the curious rock formation. He shrugged and turned away. He wasn't in that lonely country to study geology.

Once he left the mouth of the canyon, he headed swiftly back towards the camp. The sun was gone behind the western heights and a cool wind blew against his back, chilling him through his sweat-soaked shirt.

A shot flatted off as he neared the camp. The echo slammed back and forth between the heights on either side. Hugh trotted forward, cocking and capping his Sharps. Then he saw the people of the party behind the low wall where they had made their camp. Greer, the orderly, was running towards the wall with his carbine in his hands.

Hugh came up behind the camp. Stevens turned swiftly and raised his carbine, then lowered it as he saw Hugh. Greer stumbled wearily to the wall and grounded his carbine. "Apaches," he said in his high-pitched voice.

Carbines were thrust over the wall. Able Clymer took out his Colt and cocked it. He strode back and forth as though he were on the quarterdeck of a frigate going into battle.

Hugh dropped over the wall. "Get in here, Greer," he said.

Greer was helped over the wall by Stevens. His face was white with fear.

"Did you actually see an Apache?" asked Hugh.

"Yes."

Hastings spat. "He's liable to see anything."

Greer wiped the cold sweat from his narrow face. "I was on guard, Kinzie," he said nervously. "The wind was rustling on brush. Then I saw the brush move a hundred yards from me. There was something dark in amongst the brush. I shot at it."

Hugh gripped him by the shirt front. "But did you see a warrior?"

Greer looked at the people surrounding

him. Then he looked away. "Well, now I'm not so sure."

Clymer raised a big hand. "I ought to buck and gag you," he said.

"Saddle the horses," said Hugh. "Get the pack mules ready."

"Why?" asked Nettleton. He wet his lips. "If there are no Apaches out there we can spend the night here."

"You've had a full day's rest. The horses and mules are all right now. We couldn't hold this position if the Apaches got above us. First thing you'd know, they'd stampede the animals, then sit up on those heights and shoot at us. We'd be like fish in a barrel."

Phillips rubbed his jaw. "He's right."

Clymer shot a look of scorn at Phillips. "You're both as panicky as Greer."

Nettleton looked down the canyon. "What did you find, Kinzie?"

"There is a trail north of here."

Nettleton looked at his wife and then sighed deeply. "Good! Then we can make for the Rio Grande."

"No. There's no way through there

that I could find. This trail leads north-west, possibly to the San Francisco."

"We're not going that way," said Clymer.

Hugh looked at him. "Then stay here. I'm going North. If all of you want to take a chance on that trail you'd better go with me."

Nettleton nodded. "Then we must chance it."

Clymer twirled his Colt by its trigger guard, then deftly slid it into his holster. "Phillips! See to the horses."

Phillips flushed. Clymer treated him like a corporal instructing a raw recruit. Then without a word he beckoned to Willis, Pearce and Stevens, and led them to the animals.

Hugh walked south down the canyon. He stopped at the place where the guard had been. The canyon was deep in shadow. A hawk floated high overhead on a leisurely hunt for food. Suddenly he flew swiftly off to the west. There was no other sign of life down there, but there was a brooding air about the place.

Hugh scanned the brush. It moved in the wind. A more stable man than Greer would have thought something was moving about in the brush.

Hugh walked back to the camp. Roswell was saddling Hugh's buckskin. "See anything?" he asked.

Hugh shook his head.

"Greer scares easy."

"Nerves have a way of failing in this country. Maybe it's what you don't see that frightens you."

Roswell nodded. "I know what you mean."

Hugh led the buckskin to the wall. Mrs. Nettleton stood there with her shawl over her shoulders. "You'll ride all night after that hard scout up the canyon?" she asked.

Hugh took off his hat. "It's my job, Mrs. Nettleton."

She took in his broad shoulders and slim waist. Hugh was suddenly conscious of his whiskers and sweaty clothing.

"You feel better now?" he asked.

"Yes, thank you. Will it be a hard ride?"

He smiled. "Anywhere within fifty square miles around here is a hard ride."

"Will we ever reach the Rio Grande?"

He looked away. "Certainly."

She came closer. "Don't lie to me."

He looked down at her. "All right, then. It's a fifty-fifty chance. Maybe less."

She looked at her husband. He was checking the lashing on a mule pack. "Maurice is worried about me. But I'm tougher than he thinks I am."

Hugh grinned. "You should be. You're Boss Bennett's daughter, aren't you?"

She smiled. "You know of him then?"

"I'm from Missouri too."

She placed a hand on his arm. "Now I feel better. Stay close to me on the trail, Mr. Kinzie."

"I will."

He watched her walk gracefully towards her horse. Abel Clymer held its reins. He looked over her head at Hugh, and there was cold hate on his broad face.

Hugh swung up on his horse. Katy

Corse rode up to him. "I see you have the same old fascination," she said.

"What's bothering you, Katy?"

She looked at Marion Nettleton. Clymer was standing there talking to her, with a smile on his face. "Her," she said.

"Meaning?"

Katy tilted her head to one side and studied Hugh. "There are some women who like all men. They think men have been put on earth for one purpose . . . to take care of them, and them alone."

"Katy, set your mind at rest. I want to get this party to safety, then go about fighting a war. Right now I haven't got time to worry about Marion Nettleton beyond getting her to the Rio Grande." He spurred forward and left her.

"I wonder," Katy Corse said softly.

Darrell Phillips posted Willis and Stevens at the rear of the party, then rode over to Katy. "You're ready?" he asked.

She glanced at him. "As ready as I'll ever be, Mr. Phillips."

He leaned close to her. "My friends call me Darrell."

"Darrell, then."

"Thanks," he said.

They rode together at the rear of the party.

6

ANY Apache within a mile would know where the struggling party was. The thought was Hugh Kinzie's as he sat his horse by the side of the trail listening to the noisy progress up the dark canyon. Hooves clashed against rock. A mule bawled now and then. Metal clashed against metal. Men cursed. The cacophony rose up into the night and echoed loudly from the canyon walls, magnifying the din manyfold.

There would be a new moon that night, of that Hugh was sure. It would help to show the trail, but it would also show the travellers to keen Mimbreno eyes. But if they had been travelling in ink, the noises they made would reveal them to anyone.

Hugh cut a chew and stowed it into his mouth. He wanted a smoke, but knew better than to make a light. As the noise of the party was dimmed by the distance, he became aware of the natural night sounds. The moaning of the wind through the canyon. The rustling of brush. The occasional cry of a night bird.

He looked down the canyon. He was sure that sonofabitch Jorge Dura had split the wind to alert the Mimbrenos. He should have killed him with no more compunction than a mountain lion has when killing a deer. Hugh slid a hand along his cold carbine barrel. If he saw Dura with the Mimbrenos he'd break his own neck to get a bead on him.

Hugh wondered which of the men in the party he could rely on in a tight fight. He discarded Greer and Nettleton. Greer would run; Nettleton would be worried about his wife. Hastings would fight. He had guts, for all his big mouth. Stevens and Roswell would be steady. Pearce and Willis would look out for their own rumps. Isaiah Morton would be down on his knees. Phillips had a high sort of courage, in Hugh's opinion. Clymer might be the type of big bully who turns yellow when a little man stands up to him. It was all in the deck and the Apaches had marked cards.

He listened again to the night sounds. Greer might have seen an Apache. If he had, there would be more of them, probably nosing around like questing hounds at the deserted camping place.

Hugh touched the buckskin with his spurs. There was nothing but darkness behind him as he rode up the canyon, but his imagination peopled it with Mimbrenos, moving silently and swiftly on the trail.

The moon was casting a sickly pale light into the canyon when the party reached the place where the ancient trail trended north-west. Hugh called a halt. The light was good enough for them to continue on into the big canyon he had seen beyond the rock wall.

The men dismounted. Clymer helped Marion Nettleton to the ground. Katy Corse slid from her saddle and glanced at them. Nettleton bustled over to his wife, glanced angrily at Clymer, and then looked at her. "Are you all right, Marion?" he asked.

"She's fine, Captain," said Clymer.

"I didn't ask you, Abel."

Clymer shrugged and then went to his horse. He took his canteen and drank from it, watching Nettleton and his wife.

"The big stud is working overtime, as usual," said a dry voice behind Hugh.

Hugh turned. It was Chandler Willis.

"Got a chew, scout?" asked Willis.

Hugh silently handed him his plug. Willis cut off a chew and stowed it in his wide mouth. He worked it into pliability and then spat. "*Bueno!*" he said.

"Where's Pearce?"

Willis shrugged. "Somewheres. Taking care of nature's call, most likely."

"Get him. Go back down the trail. Watch and listen. For God's sake keep quiet."

Willis hitched up his gunbelt. "Shore. I been around redsticks before."

"Where?"

"Apaches, Comanches, Lipans, Kiowas, Tonks."

71

"You're from Texas?"

Willis shifted his chew and spat forcefully. "Now I didn't say that, did I?" He wandered off into the shadows. "Hey, Dan!" he called out. "Get your carbeen. We got guard."

"Again? Ain't there no other soldiers around here?"

Willis laughed. "Just you and me, sonny. *Vamos!*"

The two troopers tramped down the canyon. Hugh could hear Pearce cursing luridly as he stumbled along.

Hugh walked up to the party. "We'll follow this trail for a way yet. It's tough going, but we can get through. We'll walk from here on."

"What's up ahead?" asked Phillips.

"More canyon. It gets bigger as you go along."

"Can we get out of it?"

"I don't know."

Clymer raised his big head. "What do you mean?"

Hugh leaned against a boulder. "Just what I said."

"I don't like your lip, scout. And I don't like the idea of stumbling through these mountains on an unknown trail."

"You can always go back."

Clymer balled big hands and planted them on his hips. "Trusting one man. I don't like it. How do we know who and what you are?"

"Look in the social register," said Hugh dryly.

"Kinzie? Kinzie? You have a relative at Fort Buchanan some weeks back?"

"My brother was there for a time. Captain Ronald Kinzie."

Clymer came closer to Hugh. "That turncoat? He went over to Rebels, didn't he?"

"I don't know."

"You don't know or you won't say? Which?"

Hugh straightened up. "I said I didn't know."

Clymer raised his head. "There's something about you that doesn't ring true, Kinzie."

"So?" said Hugh quietly.

73

Clymer came closer. He glanced down at Hugh's holstered Colt. "You lead us into hell's half acre without knowing where you're going."

"I'm with you."

"Yeah," sneered Clymer. "For what reason?"

Isaiah Morton came between them. "Let us have peace," he said.

Clymer hurled him aside with one huge hand. The man hit the ground, hard. Roswell pulled him to his feet. Nettleton hurried forward. "Clymer," he said. "Stop this madness. Kinzie is doing his best."

"His best isn't good enough."

"Then I *order* you to stop!"

Clymer didn't take his eyes from Hugh. "Go back to your wife, Nettleton," he said quietly.

Nettleton flushed.

"We're all on our own here," Clymer said.

Hugh looked down at Clymer's Colt. "If you're on your own, Clymer, you'd better make your play now."

Boots clashed on the loose rock. Chandler Willis came up to the party. "We'd better get movin'," he said. "I think there are 'Paches down the gulch."

Hastings took his eyes from Clymer and Hugh. "You seeing things too, Willis?"

Willis spat. "I didn't see nothing. But I heard a horse whinny down the canyon, and we ain't left any behind, have we, Sergeant?"

Hugh looked at Nettleton. "We'd better move on," he said. "I'll have to lead the way."

Nettleton nodded nervously. "Sergeant Hastings, stay as rear guard with Pearce and Willis."

"Yes, sir."

Clymer still stood there like a bull waiting to smash a china shop. Hugh picked up his carbine. He looked at Clymer. Clymer tuned and walked to his horse.

Isaiah Morton raised his voice. "Let us be kind, one to another," he intoned. "For are we not all brothers?"

"Shut up!" said Clymer. He checked

his plump saddlebags and then led his horse up the canyon.

"Tough cob," said Jonas Stevens to Hugh. "You didn't have to worry. I had my carbine aimed at his back all the time he was chousing you."

"Thanks," said Hugh dryly.

Hugh led the buckskin past the little column. The big mesa loomed to the west, silvered by moonlight, lonely and cold-looking. He led the way over the rock slides, listening to the din behind him as hoofs clashed against rock.

The trail darkened as he entered the narrow canyon. Every instinct in Hugh Kinzie, honed by years of dangerous living, seemed to scream against going up that narrow hall of rock. It was different when an enemy could be seen and shot at; here there was nothing but the silent menace behind them. That was the worst part of it. Hugh could pull out. He'd make it somehow, afoot or on horseback. But somehow he seemed to see the calm face of Katy Corse in front of him, taking the tough trail as well as any of the men.

Hugh canted his head, listening to the sounds. High above him he could see where the moon silvered the rocks. They seemed to move and sway as the shadows of the wind-agitated brush played across them. An awful responsibility seemed to come and settle on Hugh Kinzie's shoulders, like the Old Man of the Sea who had plagued Sinbad. Hugh tried to shake off the feeling. Sinbad had been a wanderer like himself. They had a lot in common, but Sinbad had always played a lone game, looking out for his own tough rump.

It was a helluva country. It looked smooth and peaceful at a distance, like a sleeping cat. But rile the cat and the sharp claws came out from beneath the silken fur to rip and tear. Get deep into the country and feel the godawful loneliness drape itself about your shoulders. Feel the eerie qualities of the mountain night, engendered by the softly moaning wind and the shifting shadows.

The trail he was following, for instance. Who had made it? Where had they come from and where had they vanished to? They were long dead now. Hugh shook his head to drive away these thoughts. An old scout had once told him the best man for scouting in that country was a man who used his imagination to think only of liquor and women, and cut it off short when gruesome thoughts tried to worm their way into his head.

The great rock wall loomed ahead of him. He led the buckskin up the rough way. At the top he stopped and looked down. Clymer was helping Marion Nettleton up the first slope. Katy Corse was just behind them. Hugh could hear the men cursing as they tried to get the animals started up the slippery rocks.

It took them half an hour to get all the animals to the top. Hastings and his two men appeared as the last mule scrambled clumsily up to the top.

Nettleton shoved back his hat and looked into the great canyon, bathed in ghostly moonlight. "Is there water here?" he asked.

"I don't know. We'll have to ration ourselves."

"Great!" grunted Clymer.

Hastings, Pearce and Willis reached the top. All eyes surveyed the canyon. There was a quality of deep loneliness about it. When anyone spoke he unconsciously did so in a whisper, as though standing in the nave of a great cathedral.

Hugh led the buckskin down the steep slope. There was no use in telling the others to follow. They were on a one-way road.

Hugh reached the bottom when one of the mules stumbled into a hole, fell sideways, then rolled down towards Hugh. The mule bawled once, then landed heavily ten feet from Hugh.

"Damn you, Pearce!" yelled Clymer. "You did it!"

Pearce turned to look up at the officer, his face contorted. "What the hell did you want me to do, sir? Hold him back by his damned halter?"

"Damn you! I'll have you bucked and gagged! I'll string you up by your thumbs! I'll have you court-martialled! You'll be drummed out of the service to the Rogue's March!"

"You'll have crap, Clymer! That's all you'll have!"

Hastings raised his carbine. He slammed the butt between Pearce's shoulders. "That's enough out of you!"

Pearce went down head first, cracking his head against a rock. He shook his head and then felt the blood flowing down his face. He opened his mouth as he looked at Hastings. Then he shut it. But there was pure hell in his cold green eyes.

Hugh walked to the mule. It was dead. He cut the pack lashings and pulled the packs free with the help of Roswell. "Lost a good mule for this junk," said the corporal.

Nettleton stopped behind them. "Place those packs on another mule, Roswell."

Roswell turned, a strange look on his face. "Sir? Those other two mules are overloaded as it is."

"Then put them on a horse!"

"Whose?"

They were all down at the bottom of the slope now. Nettleton looked from one to the other of them and then down at the packs. "That's our silver," he said pettishly. "Our wedding gift from my father-in-law. What would he say if we left it here?"

Willis laughed softly in the background.

Hugh took his bridle reins. "Is there any food in those packs?"

Nettleton shook his head. "Just the big silver set and some of my extra uniforms packed about them. Perhaps a few dishes and some household goods."

"Good! Let it lie."

Nettleton looked at his wife. She nodded and Nettleton went to his horse . . .

Clymer was grumbling again as Hugh led the way across the canyon floor. It was still rough going because of scattered rocks and thick brush. "No water. No trail," he said. "Led by the brother of a rebel. What next?"

Stevens was beside Hugh. He looked

back. "Why don't you shut him up, Kinzie? I know you're not afraid of him. Why do you let him ride you like this? He's been doing it ever since you joined us."

Hugh looked at the trooper. "I've got a job to do, Jonas. To get this party to the Rio Grande."

"And then?" Stevens looked closely at Hugh's taut face. Hugh didn't have to tell him anything. It was written on the scout's face like a page of print.

"God help Clymer," he said softly.

7

HUGH looked back as he reached the end of the tumbled rock piles. He could see the rock wall which almost blocked the canyon. It looked like the great rock walls of the ancients. There was no sign of life on it. He had half expected to see a row of warriors standing there watching the party below them.

The wall behind him stuck in his mind as he led the buckskin through a thicket of brush. It brought back the curious even line of rock he had seen on the left wall of the canyon earlier that day. He turned and looked towards it. His jaw dropped. He stopped short.

"What is it?" asked Stevens.

Hugh swallowed dryly. "Look," he said hoarsely.

"For Pete's sake!"

Phillips came up behind them. "What

is it? Apaches?" Then he stopped and looked with wonder in his dark eyes.

The arched roof of an enormous cave extended for many yards along the face of the mesa side. Filling it was a silent city of stone built in terraces reaching back into the great cave. The moonlight bathed the mortared walls in soft light. Windows and doors stood out in the stark relief of their shadows. Here and there a round or a square tower stood up, breaking the irregular line of the tops of the main structures It looked like a brooding medieval castle transported by some magical means to the mountains of New Mexico.

The rest of the party crowded up behind them. "What's holding us up?" snapped Nettleton.

Phillips silently extended an arm to point towards the mesa wall.

"What a curious rock formation," said Marion Nettleton.

"It ain't real, is it?" asked Dan Pearce.

"I've heard of these places," said Darrell Phillips slowly. "It's a cliff dwelling."

"There anyone there?" asked Willis. He hefted his carbine.

Hastings spat. "I saw a place like that in Arizona once. Only it wasn't near as big."

Harry Roswell walked forward. "It's real enough. There's one something like it out near the Santa Cruz. The greasers call it Casa Grande."

"Who built it?" asked Katy Corse.

"The Hohokam . . . the Old Ones," said Hugh quietly. "I noticed it late this afternoon, but it was hard to see. I should have known what it was . . . those old fields we saw along the way . . . a trail where no trail should be."

They stood there in the moonlight looking up at the cliff dwelling. One of the mules suddenly brayed loudly. The echo rang from the cliff wall. Hugh turned quickly and raised his carbine.

"Shut up!" yelled Clymer at the mule.

"One jackass telling the other to shut up," said Willis.

Hugh padded back and looked towards the rock wall behind them. Mules were the best sentries there could be in Indian country. They could smell a warrior a mile away.

Something moved at the bottom of the rock wall. Hugh raised his carbine and then lowered it. He was getting as jittery as Greer. He studied the darkness at the bottom of the slope. Something had moved near the mule. Maybe a prowling coyote. There was one thing he knew for sure: Apaches loved sweet mule meat.

He backed towards the party. "Get around those rocks," he said over his shoulder.

"What is it?" asked Nettleton.

"I don't know. There's something at the bottom of the rock wall near the mule."

"My silver!"

"Damn your silver! Get moving!"

Hugh watched the place where he thought he could see the body of the mule. Hoofs clattered behind him as the horses and mules were led off the trail.

Roswell came up beside Hugh. He wet his lips. "You see 'em?"

"No."

"They there?"

"I think so."

"We can't fight out here."

"They won't attack at night."

"Yeah. But what about dawn?"

"That's it. Start the rest of them towards that cliff dwelling. Pronto!"

Hugh could hear Nettleton's peevish voice. "Why does he want us to go up there?"

"We can't hold off an attack out here in the open, sir," said Roswell.

"He's right," said Phillips.

"Supposing there are Indians up there?"

Clymer laughed. "If there are, they've been dead a couple of hundred years. No fear, Captain, unless you're afraid of ghosts."

"You try my patience, Mr. Clymer!"

Hugh backed around the rock formation and trotted after the rest of them. They made enough noise to start every sleeping echo in that great canyon into wide-awake action.

Close up under the dwellings there was a great talus slope of broken stone stippled with thorny brush. The horses shied at the slope, but the two mules slogged on. Nettleton started up the slope, dragging Marion by her arm. Katy Corse looked back at Hugh. "Are you all right?"

Hugh wiped the sweat from his face. "Yes."

Dan Pearce stood to one side staring up at the silvery dwellings. "By Joe, Chand," he said to Willis, "maybe there's treasure up in there. Gold, maybe."

Willis looked quickly at the others. "Shut up, you damned fool," he said.

They made clashing progress up the slope. Hugh came up last. The east end of the canyon seemed devoid of life. Maybe he had imagined seeing something move near the dead mule.

A crude low wall of unmortared stones ran the length of the first terrace. There was a place where it had crumbled, and through this place they led the animals on to a long flat terrace of irregularly shaped flat stones. The interstices had been filled with packed earth. Here and there along the terrace were rounded areas in the centre of which was a sort of trap door. The shafts of crude ladders projected from some of them.

The walls of the closely joined buildings were pierced with small rectangular windows and curiously shaped doors. They looked like the capital letter T, with an exceptionally wide cross bar. Here and there crude ladders still rested against the sills of upper-story doors. Sagging wooden walk-ways rested on beams which projected from the walls, forming a means of entry into second-story dwellings.

The structures, close up, now showed signs of ruin. Roofs had tumbled in, filling the interiors of the small rooms. Walls had crumbled, littering the terraces and passageways between structures. Clumps of brush had sprung up in patches of earth, and an occasional stubborn tree had rooted itself where its seed had been carried by the wind.

No one spoke. They studied the ancient

structures with questioning eyes. The silence was broken only by the stamping of one of the animals and the sighing of the wind through openings in the buildings.

Hugh at last broke away from his trance. He walked to the far end of the terrace and looked down into the moonlit canyon. A coyote howled from the heights across from the ruins. A moment later another coyote answered the first one, this time from the east end of the canyon. Hugh nodded. The Apaches were experts at animal calls, but the trained ear could detect a difference. How many of them were out there? If they were already on the far side of the canyon they could now block the way to the San Francisco. It was time to make a decision. Stay at the ruins, where they could defend themselves, or try for the only exit from the canyon. If the Apaches caught them on the canyon floor they would be wiped out. If they stayed at the ruins they would be hemmed in until hunger and thirst drove them into the open. They were damned if they did and damned if they didn't.

Darrell Phillips came along the terrace, still looking up at the ancient structures. "Amazing," he said as he reached Hugh.

"How long do you think they been here?"

"*Quién Sabe?*"

A coyote howled from far to the west. Hugh nodded. Darrell Phillips looked curiously at Hugh. "What's wrong?"

"Listen."

The wind moaned through the canyon. Minutes passed. Then from the west, on the ruins side of the canyon came a coyote howl. The net was completely around them now. The catch was in the net.

"Just a coyote," said Phillips. He laughed.

"No. Mimbrenos."

"You're sure?"

Hugh merely looked at the young officer. Phillips nodded. "I should have known better than to question you."

Phillips waved an arm at the cliff dwellings behind them. "This is a strange thing. These people were an agricultural people, probably simple and peaceful. Why would they build their city up here in a place difficult to reach when they could have built equally as well out on the flats?"

"You tell me."

"Because something drove them up here, forcing them to build a fortress to live in, as our ancestors did in the Dark Ages when bands of robbers roamed the country."

"So?"

"The Apaches are nomadic as are the Navajos. Do you suppose their ancestors forced these people to live like this?"

"It's possible."

Phillips picked up a stone and dropped it over the wall. It hit far below and then rattled down the slope. "There is a curious parallel here, Kinzie."

"Yes?"

Phillips looked across the moonlit canyon. "We've been driven up here because we too are forced to protect ourselves against nomadic brigands."

"I see what you mean."

"One other thing bothers me."

"Yes?"

Phillips looked at Hugh. "What happened to the people who lived here?"

Hugh shoved back his hat. "I see what you mean. I'll tell you this: I'm not licked yet. No damned Mimbreno is going to sit out there like a spider in his web waiting for Hugh Kinzie to blunder into it. Let's go! We've got work to do."

They walked back along the terrace. Phillips glanced at Hugh. "You knew Katy Corse pretty well before the war, didn't you?"

"You asked me that once before."

"Yes."

"Why do you ask me again?"

Phillips flushed. "I suppose I forgot."

"Don't josh me, Mr. Phillips. I have no claim on her."

Phillips smiled. "Thanks."

Hugh stopped and gripped the young officer by the arm, swinging him around easily so that he faced Hugh. "You said that time that she'd make a good wife for an enlisted man. I said she'd make a good wife for *any* man. Do I make myself clear?"

Phillips tried to pull away but the strong fingers dug into his left bicep like steel wires. "Don't threaten me, Kinzie," he said in a low voice.

Hugh released him. "I wasn't threatening you. I was just reminding you that Katy Corse is a lady, as good as any lady you've ever met, and a helluva lot more of a real woman than Marion Nettleton." Hugh strode towards the others.

Nettleton looked down into the deserted valley. "Are they out there?"

Hugh nodded. "We'll stay here until we are sure they're gone."

"How long will that be?"

"*Quién Sabe?*"

"I don't like it, Kinzie. We have very little food and water."

Hugh glanced at the two pack mules. "There might be some water. As for food . . . well, those three mules you started out with could have carried enough cold tack for a platoon."

"Sure, sure," said Clymer. "But we can't do anything about that now."

"We can do this," said Hugh quietly. "Place all food under guard and ration it. We might knock down a deer or a bear, if we're lucky. Until that time we're under short rations."

Nettleton wet his lips. "Sergeant Hastings," he said "take charge of all the food; gather the canteens. Place them in one of these small rooms and put a guard over them."

Hastings saluted. "Stevens and Greer! Come with me. Check all saddlebags, cantle and pommel packs for food."

Willis leaned against the wall. He glanced at the two pack mules. "I hope that includes Nettleton's liquor," he said. "I could do with a slug or two."

Abel Clymer walked towards his horse. He took the saddlebags. "Greer!" he said. "Check these for food."

Greer shambled over. He was scared to death of the Apaches, but he looked like he'd rather face them than Abel Clymer.

"I'm sure there isn't any food in there, sir," he said.

"Check them!" said Hugh.

Clymer flushed. He thought he had picked his man in Greer, and he had been right, but he hadn't figured on Hugh Kinzie.

Greer unbuckled one of the bags and thrust in his hands. He felt around, then drew out his hands and opened the other bag. He felt around in it. Then suddenly he looked up at Clymer with an odd expression on his face. Clymer eyed the little clerk steadily. Greer withdrew his hands and buckled the straps. "All right, sir," he said. "You're clean."

Clymer spat over the wall and hooked his saddlebags over his left arm. "Willis!" he said. "You clean out one of the rooms for Mrs. Nettleton."

"Yes, sir." Willis walked towards the row of structures. He glanced at the pack mules as he did so. A man could use a drink about now.

Hastings had the food piled up against a wall. There were about a dozen cans of embalmed beef, some slabs of dry-looking bacon, several containers of hardtack. The small amount Hugh had brought with him had been added to the pile.

"Ain't a helluva lot, is it?" asked Stevens of Hugh.

"About enough for two days if it's stretched thin."

"The Lord will provide," said Morton solemnly.

"He'd better start issuing," Pearce said.

Clymer strode over to one of the openings in the terrace floor. He tested the ladder with his hand. "Too fragile for me. Who's lightest here? You . . . Greer!"

Greer rubbed a dirty hand across his mouth. "Me . . . sir?"

Clymer nodded impatiently. "Take a look down there."

Greer walked over to the ladder and looked down into the hole. "I haven't got a light."

Clymer handed him a block of Strike Anywhere matches. Greer took them and broke one off. He drew the match across his belt buckle and held it down into the hole. It flared up in the draught. He dropped it down into the hole and stared after it. "Can't see a thing," he said.

Clymer shoved Greer towards the hole. "Go on," he said. Hugh took a picket line from a horse and walked over to Greer. He made a loop in the line and passed it over Greer's head and then under his arms. He drew the loop tight about Greer's chest. "Go on," he said.

There was naked fear on Greer's thin face. "What's down there, Kinzie?"

Hugh grinned. "A floor. It can't be a mine shaft."

"You're sure?"

"I'm not sure of anything except that I won't let go of this picket line." Hugh fastened his end of the line to his saddle, then coiled up the slack.

Clymer spat. "Get going, Greer."

The little man looked at Hugh and then at Clymer. Then he gingerly placed his feet on the ladder and began to go down. He took his time. Hugh could hear him breathing harshly as he tested each shaky rung.

Clymer shoved back his hat. "Yellow-belly," he said.

"I didn't see you racing to get down there, Clymer," said Hugh.

There was no sound from below. Then suddenly something snapped. A high-pitched scream seemed to shoot out of the hole like a rocket. Wood splintered, and there was the thump of a falling body. From the sound of it Greer hadn't fallen far. Hugh drew in on the line. The little clerk screamed again. "Give me a hand!" snapped Hugh at Clymer. They hauled Greer up, easing him through the hole. Hugh stared at Greer's face. It was a mask of blood.

Marion Nettleton screamed. "What's down there!"

Greer sank to the ground, pawing at his bloody face. Incoherent cries seemed to be pistoned out of his mouth at intervals. "It was awful!" he finally managed to gasp.

Hugh gripped Greer by the collar.

"What, you fool!" he said. "What was it you saw?"

Greer's eyes were wide in his face. "Nothing! I saw nothing! It was the feeling I had down there."

Hugh unfastened the picket line from Greer. He passed the end under his arms and lashed it. "Stevens," he said, "Feed out the slack as I go down."

Hugh went down into the darkness, feeling out with his legs as he went down. It was only a short distance. He hit hard earth with his feet and drew down a little slack from the line. He lit a match and looked about. The flickering light of the big match revealed a circular room, perhaps twenty feet across. A low shelf completely encircled the wall, and from it rose a number of low pilasters which held up the roof. The shelf was supported by an ingenious framework of cribbed logs covered with the hard earth of the terrace.

Hugh lit another match. The packed floor had been sprayed by the blood from Greer's nose. An eerie feeling came over Hugh as he stood there. He pulled at the picket line, then raised himself hand over hand until he pulled himself out on to the terrace. He looked at the other. "Nothing down there," he said.

Greer was wiping his face. "No? Maybe something you can't see, but there's something down there, Kinzie, and you know it. I can see it in your eyes!"

Some of the onlookers were nervous. Others stood there with drawn faces. There was something about the whole occurrence which had triggered strange thoughts in their minds. The whole place had an eerie, haunting quality about it, as though unseen eyes were always watching them.

Willis crawled out of a room. "Got it fairly well cleaned out," he said. "Lotsa trash in there. Mrs. Nettleton, you'll be all right in there."

Nettleton looked at Greer. "Get Mrs. Nettleton settled in there. For God's sake, get the rest of that blood off of your face." Nettleton turned towards Clymer. "Form a guard, Mr. Clymer."

Clymer looked at Phillips. "Take over, Mr. Phillips," he said shortly.

Later, as Hugh carried his blankets into one of the shelters which still boasted a roof, he looked out along the terrace. Stevens was pacing back and forth at the far end. Pearce leaned against a wall at the other end. The horses had been unsaddled and the mules unloaded. From somewhere in one of the small rooms he could hear a strident snoring. There was no sign of life in the canyon.

Hugh straightened out his blankets. Harry Roswell raised his head from where he was lying. "You think they'll bother us?" he asked.

Hugh pulled off his boots. "Not likely. Unless we try to leave. They don't like these places. Places Of The Dead, they call them. They'll bide their time until we're ready to pull out."

"Then we'll get it."

"Maybe . . . maybe not."

Hugh dropped on his blanket and looked up at the dim ceiling of the little dwelling. He wondered how many years had passed since the builders of the room had slept there.

Roswell rolled over and looked again at Hugh. "What happened to Greer down there?" he asked quietly.

"Nerves."

"You feel anything down there?"

"No."

Roswell rubbed his jaw. "You looked a little pale when you came up."

Hugh rose up on an elbow. "Look, Harry. I don't like this place. I don't like the deal we're in. But I'm not going to lie awake talking about ghosts, if that's what you mean."

Roswell lay back and covered his eyes with his right arm. "Sorry, Hugh," he said.

The wind moaned through the little window and small doorway. It sighed along under the great arch of the cave high above the cliff-dwelling ruins. From somewhere down the canyon a coyote howled softly.

8

HUGH was up at dawn. He shivered in the cold wind as he stepped out on to the terrace. Roswell was on guard with Greer. Hugh rolled a smoke and handed the makings to Roswell. "How did it go, Harry?"

Roswell looked out over the dim canyon. He shrugged. "As quiet as the grave."

Hugh grinned. "A neat comparison."

Roswell lit his smoke. "Greer is acting peculiar."

"What's wrong?"

"Something has cracked inside of him."

Hugh nodded. "I've been expecting it. I'm going to look around."

Hugh glanced at Greer as he walked behind the little clerk. Greer was standing at the edge of the terrace, looking off into the dimness of the canyon, mumbling softly to himself.

Hugh worked his way over a pile of debris in a passageway between two dwellings. High above him the arched roof of the great cave showed darker streaks of deep red. They blended into black splotches where the cave roof ended. The streaks were at almost regular intervals and Hugh finally deduced that the smoke from the fires had discoloured the reddish-brown rock.

There was a triangular space behind the back walls of the last row of dwellings, forming a long passageway between the walls and the slanting roof of the cave. It was littered with trash. Hugh picked up a finely shaped pottery bowl decorated with a black-on-white design.

Hugh walked east the length of the passageway. It ended against the blank wall, stained by the smoke of ancient fires. He walked back the other way, feeling the utter loneliness of the place. He picked up a square of yucca matting, pieces of pottery and a flint arrowhead.

Then he was at the western end of the passageway. Here there was a semi-circular area, littered with ears of dried corn. There was a great vault in the cave wall, forming a narrow V-shaped crack in the rock. It had been carefully filled with mortared rock. Hugh skirted the crumbling wall at the end of the passageway, and eased his way through a narrow door into the bottom floor of a square, three storied tower. A notched chicken ladder rose up to the next floor. Hugh climbed up to the second story. There was no ladder leading up to the third story, but he was able to stand on a pile of debris, grasp the edges of the trap door, and pull himself up into the top story. The roof had fallen in at one side. The light of early morning came in through a window, and flooded in through the gap in the roof.

Hugh walked over to the window, and standing well back from it, he looked out over the canyon. The tower afforded a fine place to watch the whole area in front of the ruins. There wasn't a sign of life on the brushy floor of the canyon. Hugh looked across to the far wall. He could have sworn the brush at one point moved a little against the wind.

Hugh rolled a smoke and studied the canyon. A good rifleman in the tower could sweep the slopes in front of the ruins. He knew they could hold the ruins against fifty Mimbrenos. But would the Mimbrenos attack? It was a place of the dead, and their superstitious fears would work on them enough to keep them at a distance. But they could let the lack of food and water drive the White-eyes from the ruins. It shouldn't take long.

Hugh looked along the terrace below him. Willis was kindling a fire from shattered roof poles. Stevens was filling a large coffee-pot with water from a canteen. Greer was squatted against the front of a dwelling, his thin hands hanging down in front of his knees. Morton was on the terrace just below the tower with his battered Bible in his hands.

Katy Corse came out of one of the

dwellings. She swept back her long hair with her hands, and thrust a comb into one side of the deep black tresses. She walked to the edge of the terrace and stood there, breathing deeply of the fresh morning air. Hugh thought that Katy Corse would be at home anywhere.

Darrell Phillips walked towards Katy. She laughed as he said something. They stood there together looking out towards the canyon, almost as though they were safe in some park back in the East.

Dan Pearce came out between two buildings, looked up and down the terrace, then furtively ducked back into a passageway again. First Sergeant Hastings was checking over the small stock of food, shaking his head as he did so. Harry Roswell was inspecting the horses picketed along the terrace.

Captain Nettleton came out of the room in which he had spent the night. "Is that coffee ready, Stevens?" he called out.

"No, sir."

"Hurry it up."

"The fire isn't hot enough, sir."

Nettleton threw his hands up in petty anger. He looked into the room he had just left. "It won't take long, dear," he said.

Hugh thought of the lack of water. Maybe he should stop Stevens from making the coffee. But he had stuck his neck into enough bickering already, without going so far as to deprive them of their morning coffee.

Hugh dropped down to the second floor of the tower. There was a startled exclamation from the first floor, then the crush of boots against the debris-littered floor. Hugh looked down through the opening. The first floor was empty. He turned on a heel and jumped to a side window, looking down into the narrow passageway between the wall and the end wall of the great cave. It was empty. But he did see something. Across from him was a rock shelf, slanting down and away from him. There was a thin trickle of moisture glistening against the wall.

Hugh pulled up the chicken ladder and thrust it across the gap between the tower and the rock shelf. He teetered across. There was a shallow pan of water there, hardly enough to wet the rock. There was a slow dripping from the trickle against the wall. Hardly enough water to keep one person alive for long, much less thirteen. "Thirteen!" he said aloud.

He walked back across the ladder and replaced it where he had found it. He'd keep the knowledge of the water to himself for a time, until he figured out. what to do. He passed back into the triangular passageway. It was empty of life.

Hugh walked out on the terrace. Abel Clymer appeared at the far end and glanced at Hugh, then he came towards the fire. Hastings was doling out the meat and hardtack. "Willis," he said, "you and Pearce take morning guard."

Willis stopped with his meat half-way to his wide mouth. "Hell, Sarge! I was on four hours last night."

"We're not running this outfit from a duty roster."

Willis glanced at Phillips, at Clymer

and then at Hugh. "There's some here had a full night's sleep," he said.

Hugh leaned against a wall. "We can get by with one guard during the day," he said. "Send him to that tower at the west end. He can see the whole terrace, the slope, and a good part of the canyon from up there. Good field of fire."

Clymer's eyes held Hugh's for a moment, then the big officer turned away. "Captain Nettleton," he said loudly, "how long are we going to stay here?"

Nettleton put down his coffee cup. "Until we're sure there are no Apaches out there," he said.

Clymer laughed. "We haven't seen any yet. Maybe there aren't any out there."

"Walk down the slope," said Hugh. "Take a little stroll up or down the valley. If you don't come back then you'll know they're out there."

"I don't like this," said Clymer. He looked at Hastings. "Send out a man to look around."

Hastings stood up. He wiped his big hands on his thighs. "One man, sir?"

"Did you expect to send a squad?" asked Clymer sarcastically.

Hugh rolled a smoke. He eyed Clymer. "Ask for a volunteer, Hastings," he suggested.

The men looked away. Hastings wet his cracked lips. "Any volunteers?" he asked uncertainly. No one spoke up.

Hugh shifted a little. "You've got two good junior officers here, Captain Nettleton. A good officer wouldn't send a man on a detail he wouldn't take on himself."

Clymer scowled. Phillips went pale beneath his tan. Nettleton stood up and placed his coffee cup on a rock. "Why, yes," he said brightly. "That's it! Mr. Clymer, you and Mr. Phillips decide between yourselves who is to go."

Clymer looked at Phillips. "You go," he said.

Phillips felt about in his trousers pocket. "We'll flip for it," he said quietly.

Clymer spat. "Forget it. Forget the whole thing!" He stamped off down the terrace.

Willis softly laughed as he picked up his carbine and walked towards the tower to stand guard.

The heat of the afternoon seemed to hang in the silent canyon like a thick issue blanket. There wasn't a breath of wind. Nothing stirred. The sky was a pitiless blue, without even a cloud to suggest shelter against the blazing sun.

Hugh was in the tower, studying the far wall of the canyon with his field glasses, feeling the sticky sweat rolling down his sides. He lowered the glasses and wiped the misted eyepieces with his bandanna. Now and then one of the horses whinnied pitifully, to be answered by the dry braying of a mule. Something scraped below Hugh. He turned and looked at the opening in the floor.

There was a rattling noise from the first story. Hugh cased his glasses and walked softly to the opening. He looked down through both openings. Harsh breathing came up to him. Hugh moved. A piece of stone rolled over the edge of the opening and dropped on the chicken ladder which was between the first and second stories. Boots crushed against debris.

Hugh leaped over to the side window of the tower. He thrust his head through the window. Dan Pearce looked up at him. "What's on your mind, Dan?" asked Hugh.

Pearce flushed. "Water," he said.

"You'll have to wait."

"Willis says there's water around here somewhere."

"There is. But it isn't in that first floor room."

Pearce looked down. "Hell," he said. "I thought there might be something a man could pick up and take along with him."

"Such as?"

"Gold, maybe."

Hugh grinned. "These people were farmers, Pearce."

Pearce squinted his eyes as he looked up. "You find anything?"

"Pottery. Arrowheads. Matting. That's all."

"They must have had something of value."

Abel Clymer entered the passageway. He stared at Pearce. "What are you doing in here?"

Pearce straightened up. "I'm next on guard, sir."

"Then get up in that tower!"

Pearce glanced sideways at the big officer. He entered the tower and came up beside Hugh. "Sonofabitch," he said. "He's been poking around these ruins himself. Always was looking for something to lay his hands on back at Fort Ayres."

"Such as?"

"Money. Women. Liquor. What else is there?"

Hugh handed Pearce the glasses. "Keep away from the water," he said.

Pearce glanced out of the side window. "Ain't enough there to wet a blotter," he growled.

"Just the same . . . leave it alone."

Pearce spat dryly as Hugh went down through the opening.

Clymer was still in the passageway. He eyed Hugh. "You've got influence with the captain," he said. "Get him to give us orders to move on."

"We've been through this before."

Clymer flushed. "Mrs. Nettleton isn't standing this heat too well."

"Who is?"

Clymer gripped Hugh by the shirt front and drew him close. "Damn you! Don't get me riled, Kinzie!"

Hugh dropped his carbine butt on one of Clymer's feet. Clymer grunted in pain and stepped back. The carbine muzzle prodded the big officer in the belly. "Get out of my way," said Hugh softly.

Clymer limped backwards. His eyes were filled with feral hate as he watched Hugh walk out on to the terrace. A soft laugh came from high above Clymer. He looked up to see the grinning face of Dan Pearce. "Damn you, Pearce!" said Clymer. "I won't take anything from *you*!"

Pearce shoved a stone over the edge of the window. It hit Clymer on the head.

Clymer clawed for his Colt but Pearce leisurely rested his carbine barrel on the bottom of the window. He cocked the hammer. His eyes met Clymer's. Clymer released his hold on his pistol and limped back into the passageway. Pearce touched the partially healed scar on his head, then spat dryly down into the passageway.

9

MYRON GREER sat in a narrow space between two buildings. It was shadowy in there, but it was still hot. He could feel the sweat running down his thin body. He ran his tongue about inside his dry mouth. But it wasn't water he wanted; he needed something far stronger than that.

Strange thoughts went through Myron Greer's mind. He felt as though he should get up and walk to the edge of the terrace, climb over the wall, then slide down the slope to the vast canyon floor. Somewhere out there he might find a drink.

Maybe the scout, Hugh Kinzie, had a bottle. Those men usually had one, although they didn't drink when they worked. Too dangerous. But it was handy for cleansing wounds and easing their pain.

Above him a lizard scuttled about,

dropping bits of mortar down on Greer's bare head. He didn't move.

Maybe the people who had built these crazy cliff dwellings had learned how to ferment corn. But these people had been gone for generations. Anything they had left would have been long dried up by now. Still, if it had been well sealed and buried in the ruins, there might be a little bit of it left, and it would have a wallop like a dose of canister.

Greer raised his head. A hammer started thudding inside his skull while an iron band seemed to tighten around the outside of it. He looked out across the canyon. He didn't see the far wall shimmering and waving in the heat, but rather he saw a whirling, greyish mass, which seemed to form itself into a cone, like the inside of a whirlpool. It seemed as though he could run to the edge of the terrace and dive into the whirlpool to be swept away into its cool depths.

Abel Clymer walked up and down the triangular passageway behind the ruins. It was a little cooler in there, or so it seemed. His right instep throbbed where that sonofabitch Kinzie had dropped the steel-shod butt of his Sharps. Kinzie's time would come, but Clymer wasn't ready to get rid of him yet. Clymer wanted to get out of this hell hole and take Marion Nettleton with him. He wet his thick lips as he thought of Marion Nettleton. "Hell," he said softly.

If he could get her back to the Rio Grande and show up at Santa Fe with her, he'd be the biggest damned hero in the Southwest. With rapid promotions the order of the day, he, Abel Johnston Clymer, first lieutenant, United States Cavalry, could ask for anything. With Bennett behind him he might eventually get a brigade. General Clymer! That was the ticket!

Clymer stopped at the far end of the passage and wiped the sweat of heat and ambition from his broad face. Maurice Nettleton was in his way. Nettleton had money. That was why Clymer had stayed his little game until he had found a stake for himself. Well, he had it now. The next thing to do was to get Nettleton to move out of there, one way or another. With Kinzie to guide him, Clymer could break through. It might not be easy to get rid of Kinzie, but that job had to be done too. Then it would be Santa Fe, and the plaudits of the department commander. Then on to St. Louis and the firm, friendly handclasps of Boss Bennett. Despite the clinging heat, Clymer shivered a little in his ecstasy. "Captain Clymer. Major Clymer. Colonel Clymer. *General Clymer!*" he said aloud.

Dan Pearce peered through Hugh Kinzie's field glasses. He studied the east end of the canyon. Somewhere in the haze was that damned dead mule with Nettleton's silver still in the packs. Dan had seen the silver service back at Fort Ayres. It wouldn't take a man long to get back to that stinking mule and cut those packs loose. He could cache the silver and come back for it some day. Maybe he and Chandler Willis could make a break for the river, but there wasn't enough value

121

in the silver for two to share it. The thing to do was get the silver, hide it, then talk Willis into going out of the canyon with him. Two would have a better chance than one. Three could make it without too much trouble—if the third man was Hugh Kinzie.

Darrell Phillips looked down at his Wellington boots. Made by Bascomb of London. The best boots in the whole department, and he had to wear them into this country. The boots were scuffed, and one of them had a slit clear through the fine leather. No amount of polishing and buffing would ever make these boots look like anything worthwhile again.

Phillips closed his eyes and leaned back against the warm wall of the little room he shared with Clymer. He wrinkled his nose a little. Abel Clymer carried an animal-like odour about with him even when he was freshly scrubbed. Clymer had given him nothing but hell from the first day he had showed up at Fort Ayres. According to regulations both Abel Clymer and Darrell Phillips were officers and gentlemen. Their commissions had made them both officers. The difference between the two of them was that Abel Clymer had reached the miraculous estate of being a gentleman by the act of becoming an officer, while Darrell Phillips had been born a gentleman and would die as one.

Phillips thought of Katy Corse. She would have been as much out of place in his mother's drawing-room as Abel Clymer would have been, but there was something refreshing about her, despite her easy frontier manners. Somehow she had been able to ease the pain of his bitter loneliness. She was attractive and well formed . . . He shuddered a little as he thought of bringing her home to his mother.

He stood up and picked up his hat. Katy was outside somewhere. He had to see her, to talk with her.

Chandler Willis slitted his eyes as he looked out over the canyon. Damned if he had seen any Apaches, but he knew as well as the big scout did, that they were there. Lying in the brush on the heights across the canyon; maybe even up on the mesa which rose above the cliff dwellings. Willis had almost made his break back there when they had found the smashed remains of Winston's cattle-herding detail. He could have maybe made his way to the Rio Grande alone, then south to join Baylor's Second Texas Rifles at La Mesilla. But two men had been watching him: Lieutenant Clymer and First Sergeant Hastings. Either one of them would have shot him if they had figured he was going to desert to the Confederacy.

Chandler Willis cursed his luck. He had killed a man back on the South Llano in the fall of '59, and had made it across the Rio Grande the range of a rifleshot ahead of the dead man's relatives. From there he had drifted to Fort Bliss, where he had enlisted for a winter's feed and shelter. Hastings had tagged him with the nick-name Snowbird because of that.

Willis shifted and spat again. That damned Yankee Pearce was up to something crooked. He needed Chandler Willis for something. Something for Pearce's profit, not Willis's. Yankees were all alike.

He wondered how loyal Hugh Kinzie was. He was tough enough to be a real Tejano. Maybe he was thinking of joining the Confederacy. The two of them together could clean out this bunch of Yankees, and ride like kings into La Mesilla with a mess of rifles and equipment, plus some damned good horse and mule flesh.

Maurice Nettleton looked down at his sleeping wife. Sweat dewed her oval face. Her soft lips were parted, showing her even white teeth. Her breasts swelled against the material of her travelling dress. Nettleton swallowed hard. A cold greenish wave of fear flowed through him as he thought of losing her.

She had made him. He had been an obscure second Lieutenant of dragoons at

Jefferson Barracks when he had met her and had instantly fallen in love. He had come from a fairly well-to-do family, which made it possible for him to court her. Shelton Bennett had always said he wanted a son-in-law as tough in the rump as he was, but it wasn't really the truth, for Shelton Bennett ruled everybody who would allow him to. And his daughter, too, for all her soft looks, was as hard as nails. She had married young Maurice Nettleton because she had thought he was the kind of a man she could mould to fit her needs. Her judgement had been faulty.

Their first years of married life had been like a dream. Living in the fine big house in St. Louis; having his promotion come through years ahead of time; getting assigned to department headquarters as a staff officer. Then Shelton Bennett had quarrelled with somebody in the War Department. It had been enough to have Maurice transferred to godforsaken Arizona. The pain had been assuaged a little by his promotion to captain. Marion had looked on the affair as a gay adventure. But Maurice had been badly shaken. The country was too big and dangerous. He'd had no experience with these hard-bitten frontier soldiers. Abel Clymer, who had run Fort Ayres before, listened to Maurice with some respect, but he still ran the post. Then the slow realization had come over Maurice that Clymer was making a strong play for Marion. He was solicitous with her, and used every opportunity to show up Maurice.

Maurice Nettleton began to fan his wife. He could hear Abel Clymer's bull voice in the next room, where he was riding Darrell Phillips. Nettleton looked at the fine engraved Colt pistol in his holster, one of a pair presented to him by Shelton Bennett. Nettleton felt his hands tremble. He hated violence and bloodshed. All he wanted to do was get his wife to safety, then get himself assigned to a staff job where he could be beside his wife when she needed him. But if Abel Clymer stood in the way, he would see that

Maurice Nettleton would fight for his own.

Matt Hastings pulled his soggy shirt up over his head and swabbed his armpits with it. He had a fresh shirt in his pommel pack, but he had been saving that for his entry into Sante Fe. In twenty years' service he had bucked his way up through the ranks by his ability to follow orders, and always look like a soldier. There had been a time when the diamond of a top soldier was all he desired, but the rumours of war changed Matt Hastings' ambitions. For the first time in his army career he began to think of wearing shoulder straps instead of chevrons. Instead of obeying his officers' orders implicitly he had begun to think that perhaps he knew more than they did. He had begun to burn the midnight oil reading every military book he could lay his hands on. Matt knew them all by heart, which was a hell of a lot more than that bumbling Captain Nettleton could say, or Abel Clymer with his big mouth, or Darrell Phillips with his sensitive face and fine manners.

Matt wiped off his carbine and pistol. He'd hold this J Company outfit together if it was the last thing he ever did.

The sun had died in the west, weltering in rose and gold. Purple and black shadows mantled the mountains. A cooling wind crept out of the hills and rustled the brush.

Jonas Stevens walked along the line of thirsty horses. They had been jerking at their picket lines. Jonas touched his cracked lips with his tongue. He had saved his ration of water for that day, but there wasn't enough for one of the animals. The lack of water was one of the many things he had never figured on when he had asked for duty in the Southwest. Not for himself, but for the animals. It was different back East. Plenty of good water and fine grazing for cavalry mounts. Jonas patted the nose of one of the horses. He looked down into the dim canyon. Maybe there was water down there somewhere. Kinzie hadn't said so, but Kinzie was a secretive sort. But if there was water down there, Jonas Stevens would see to it that the horses and mules got to it.

Harry Roswell was standing his guard shift in the tower. He looked down at his two stripes. He wore them because he always obeyed orders without question, even those of a corporal who was senior to him. Matt Hastings had once said that seniority amongst corporals and second lieutenants was like virtue amongst whores, but Matt Hastings was a capable first sergeant worth half a dozen green officers.

Roswell touched his two stripes and then straightened his hat. He gripped his carbine and threw back his shoulders. His seniors could rely on him to carry out their orders. He dropped through the opening in the floor and felt about for the chicken ladder.

It was pitch dark in the canyon. A coyote howled. The wind moaned through the chasm, rustling the brush, and haunting the cliff-dwelling ruins with ghostly whisperings. Something moved furtively at the wall that edged the front of the terrace. A man rolled over the wall and landed softly on the slope. He lay there a while, listening to the night. Then he eased his way down the slope until he reached the brush at the bottom. Then he was gone through the brush, heading for the east end of the canyon.

Isaiah Morton sat in the darkness of a tumbledown room, with his back and head pressed against the warm wall. His Bible lay open on his lap, and one of Isaiah's spatulate fingers rested on the page. It was too dark to read, but it really didn't matter, for he knew the book by heart. He was sure that God had placed him in his present company for some obscure but righteous reason of His own. They were an ungodly lot. Their passions and desires were close to the surface. There was no inner peace in any of them. Some of them laughed at Isaiah Morton, but he had taken it as part of his martyrdom, part of the task which had been given to him for a vision. For Isaiah Morton had been picked to bring Christianity to Mangus Colorado. It had been said that an old priest had tried to do so many years before. But he had failed. Some said that Father Font had been a good man, and had failed not because of anything he had done, or had not done, but rather because his own people had betrayed Mangus Colorado.

The scout, Hugh Kinzie, a hard and violent man, had said the Mimbrenos were waiting for their chance out in the darkness. When that chance came they would strike and kill. Isaiah tried to conjure up a picture of Mangus Colorado. "He sitteth in the lurking places of the villages; in the secret places doth he murder the innocent; his eyes are privily set against the poor." Isaiah Morton stood up and paced back and forth. "He lieth in wait secretly as a lion in his den: he lieth in wait to catch the poor: he doth catch the poor, when he draweth him into his net." Isaiah's harsh voice rang out, echoing from the walls. "He croucheth, and humbleth himself, that the poor may fall by his strong ones!"

Someone called out along the terrace. Isaiah's voice died away. A faint murmuring echo came from the arched rock wall high above the cliff dwellings. Cold sweat bathed Isaiah's gaunt body.

From somewhere in the darkness a dry voice spoke up. "If them Apaches didn't hear that, they're deaf. He's a shoutin' minister, that man is."

Isaiah bowed his head in prayer.

Marion Nettleton was still tired. She had had more rest than anyone else in the party, and had been exposed to the least amount of hardships. She lay awake in the darkness, trying to imagine she was in her big bed in the cosy room in her father's castellated monstrosity of a house back in Missouri. She had a strong will, and a fine imagination, but she could not fight back the eerie darkness of the ruins, always pressing in for every advantage.

Maurice was outside somewhere bumbling about, trying to play the part of the frontier soldier. Maurice had always been good to her. She had fallen in love with him, or thought she had, because he had had all the outward manifestations of the kind of man she wanted, but time and closer acquaintance had showed her how wrong she had been. He was on the defensive with her now, catering to her every wish, pampering and petting her, when she had hoped for a man like her father, who ruled women, and everyone else for that matter, with a will of iron.

Marion had come west with Maurice, hoping that he would assert himself and build up a reputation, but unfortunately he had been too long under the hard thumb and the strong will of Shelton Bennett. They hadn't been at Fort Ayres more than a month when it was obvious his men were laughing at him. Mother Nettleton was his nick-name behind his back. Marion often had wondered what they called her behind her back until one day she had overheard two noncoms talking together about her. She had not been mentioned by name. "The Little Corporal", one of them had said.

Marion hadn't been too nervous when they had left Fort Ayres. Now doubt had a firm hold on Marion Nettleton. She had depended on these people for her comforts; now she was dependent on them for her very life. Maurice had bungled as usual. If he had abandoned the beef herd he would not have lost the largest part of his company, as well as the services of a skilled Indian fighter. If he had moved swiftly towards the Rio Grande, instead of travelling almost leisurely for the comfort of his wife, he might have escaped the net cast about him by Mangus Colorado. Now he was more concerned about his wife's little desires than about the dangers surrounding them. Hot coffee, a soft place to sleep, warm blankets in the cool nights, and cold water during the hot days: none of those things would matter if a screaming horde of bloodthirsty Apaches came down on them and ripped Marion's clothes from her, and ripped the ivory citadel of her shapely body with greasy hands.

Marion sat up and slowly fixed her hair. She had once thought Abel Clymer was the man to save her. At first she had hated the scout, Hugh Kinzie, with his sharp orders and bitter eyes. But Hugh Kinzie could save her if anyone could. Marion stood up and brushed her clothing. There would be a moon that night. He had once promised to stay close to her on the trail. This night she would give him his chance. Not too much, just enough to set the hook in tightly.

There was a faint suggestion of the moon in the eastern sky. Dan Pearce looked back over his shoulder. He could just make out the cliff dwellings up on the slope behind him. No one had followed him. It would be quite some time before that three-striped bastard Sergeant Hastings missed him. By that time Dan would have the silver service and any other loot from the mule packs, cached away.

Dan padded through the brush. It was almost like the old days back at Five Points when he had prowled the streets looking for drunks to smash and pluck. He looked up at the high walls of the canyon. It was almost like walking through a narrow street in New York, between rows of sagging tenements. Dan Pearce would make it all right. He had the luck and the guts.

Katy Corse slowly hooked up the front of her dress. The heat of the day was long gone and a cool wind whispered up the canyon. She wanted a bath and clean clothing, but she cast the thought from her mind. There was hardly enough water for drinking purposes, and the only women's clothing available belonged to Marion Nettleton. She hadn't offered Katy the use of any of it.

Katy walked out on to the dim terrace. There was a brooding quiet about the canyon. She could feel, rather than see, the men of the little party, staring out into the dimness and listening to every night sound. She had been through experiences like this before. At Tubac she had lived through an attack when she had been fifteen years old. Her mother had been killed in that one. In 1858 her father had been the sutler at Fort Buchanan, and Katy had helped him. Two years later he had been killed by Apaches while bringing in supplies. Katy had turned over the sutler's store to Cass Wilkerson. Cass had kept her on as his clerk. It was then she had met Hugh Kinzie.

Katy felt the breeze cool her warm flesh. She had fallen hard for Hugh Kinzie, probably because he hadn't paid much attention to her on a post where every trooper, one way or another, honestly or dishonestly, had tried to gain her favour. Hugh Kinzie was a great deal like his brother Ronald. Strangely enough, Katy had been interested in Captain Kinzie, but he had paid no more attention to her than he had to his horse or dog. Hugh seemed to have been a little more human, but still had that Kinzie aloofness about him.

Herbert Oglesby had played up his suit vigorously to Katy about the same time Hugh had seemed to be a little interested. Katy liked Herbert and had used him to place a little jealously in Hugh Kinzie, to see what he'd do. Katy had overplayed her hand, for Hugh had shied away like a badly broken horse. In common with most of the men on the post, he had assumed she was Herbert's woman. Nothing she could do, within reason, had changed Hugh's coldness towards her. Herbert had proposed. She had accepted, hoping Hugh at last would do something. He hadn't. One day he was there; the next day he was gone into the hazy mountains. A month later Herbert Oglesby had died with a flint arrowhead buried in his chest.

Katy walked to the edge of the terrace. Somehow, every time she tried to be nice to Hugh, she put her foot into it. Hugh was feisty, and had to be handled with a fine touch, and Katy Corse seemed to lack that touch.

A man came up behind Katy. She

139

turned quickly, hoping it was Hugh. She looked up into the dim face of Darrell Phillips. There wasn't any hesitation in him. He swept her close and pressed his lips against hers. She was so surprised, there was no fight in her.

"If you're going to dally," a dry voice said behind them, "you better get off the skyline. The moon is coming up."

Phillips released her and turned quickly to look into the amused face of Hugh Kinzie. "You've no right to come up on us like this!" snapped Phillips.

Hugh looked out into the canyon. "You're close enough to that slope for a Mimbreno to come upon you and have a knife into your back before you'll even smell his stink."

Phillips raised a hand. He stepped forward.

Hugh smiled. "Don't do anything you'll be sorry for, Mr. Phillips."

Phillips lowered his hand. In front of Katy Corse, he wanted desperately to prove he was a man but not at the expense of fighting Hugh Kinzie.

Hugh raised his head. "You'll be on guard tonight. We'll all take turns. The enlisted men are getting tired of doing all the work. We're all in this. We'll have to forget about rank for a while."

"All right, Kinzie."

Hugh looked at Katy. "Don't get too far from any of the men, Katy." He turned and walked away into the darkness like a great lean cat.

Darrell Phillips looked at Katy. "What did he mean by that?"

She looked away. Her hands closed into tight little fists. "Damn you," she said hotly. "Get away from me!"

Phillips reached out a hand towards her, hesitated, then turned on a heel and walked away.

A blanket of silence seemed to have settled over the great canyon. Even the wind had died away. It was almost as though the canyon was waiting for something to happen.

10

CAPTAIN NETTLETON had called a council of war. Pressures were working within him. Clymer was bullying him. Phillips certainly wasn't looking up to him. But most of the pressure came from Marion. She had a way of letting a man know how she felt about him without even opening her mouth.

Maurice paced back and forth in front of the watch-tower. Hugh Kinzie leaned against the tower wall. Abel Clymer squatted beside the terrace wall with his huge hands dangling between the frayed knees of his trousers. Darrell Phillips alone stood straight up, with squared shoulders, his hands folded together in front of him.

Nettleton plucked at his lower lip. "Gentlemen," he said hesitantly. "We must decide on a plan. Our food is almost gone. There's hardly enough water for us, and the animals are in bad shape for lack of it. Another day of this heat and they'll all be dead."

"Apaches don't attack at night," said Abel Clymer. "What's to prevent us from stripping away all excess equipment and making a try to get out of here?"

Then Darrell Phillips spoke up. "Perhaps we could make a sortie against the Mimbrenos. Say half a dozen good men could leave here when the moon is gone and climb up the canyon wall to strike the Mimbrenos in their camp."

Nettleton looked at Hugh pleadingly. Hugh shifted his chew and spat leisurely.

Nettleton paced back and forth. "Both suggestions are good. Perhaps, by combining them, we can work out an effective means of escape."

"Such as?" asked Hugh quietly.

Nettleton turned. "We can lighten the loads of the horses and mules. Some of us can remain here with the women. Others, capably led, can attack the Mimbrenos, thus diverting them from those of us who are down here. While the Mimbrenos are being diverted, the women can be started for safety. Then, when the women have a good start, those who have been holding the Mimbrenos, can follow the main party, covering their retreat until we're out of the canyon."

Chandler Willis was on guard up in the watchtower. Hugh heard the trooper shuffle his feet, then spit hard against the cave wall a few feet from the side window of the tower. Hugh didn't have to see Willis's face to know how it looked.

Nettleton was now fully taken up with his masterful plan, carried away by the way the pieces of the plan fell together neatly and surely. "We will divide into two parties. The attacking party will, of course, be led by one of us. One of us must take charge of the main party here. A man of judgement, who can gauge the precise time to move out."

"That leaves two of us," said Hugh dryly.

Nettleton hesitated. This was the crucial time. His plans always appeared well on paper, but getting men, those creatures of varied impulses and emotions to follow his cleanly outlined plans had always been the problem of Maurice Nettleton. He straightened up. After all, he *was* the commanding officer. "I will take personal command of the main party with Mr. Phillips as my aide. The main party will, of course, include the ladies, Sergeant Hastings, Corporal Roswell, Private Stevens and Mr. Isaiah Morton."

Abel Clymer raised his big head and stared at Nettleton.

Nettleton looked away. "Mr. Clymer will lead the attacking party, with Mr. Kinzie as scout. The party will consist of Privates Willis, Pearce and Greer."

There was a soft whistle from up in the tower. "Jehoshaphat," said Chandler Willis.

Abel Clymer got to his feet and cracked the knuckles of his hand. "As senior officer, Captain Nettleton, I, rather than Mr. Phillips, should be with the main party."

Phillips raised his head. "The captain has given his orders," he said.

Clymer whirled. "So? Maybe you talked him into it? I've got a good mind to break your damned jaw, Phillips!"

Phillips dropped his hand to his holstered Colt. Clymer moved in close and gripped the younger officer by the shirt front. "You haven't got the guts to pull that gun on me," he snarled. "Admit it! You talked Nettleton into taking you instead of me!"

Nettleton bustled forward. "Clymer! I'm in command here!"

Hugh stood up straight and spat his wad of chewing tobacco over the terrace wall.

"You're the big man around here," said Phillips softly. "Show Marion Nettleton what a *real* big man you are by protecting the rest of us, Clymer."

Clymer slashed a big hand across Phillips' face. Phillips jerked back his head. Clymer swung him about and rammed his back up against the tower wall. "Damn you! I'll protect her, all right! While you're out there holding back those Apaches!"

Hugh pushed Nettleton aside. He drew out his Colt and cocked it. He rammed the muzzle into Clymer's back. "Come on, stud," he said. "Lay off the heroics. The whole damned plan stinks in the first place. We're not going through with it."

Clymer released Phillips. He turned his head to look into Hugh's shadowy face. "You haven't got the guts to shoot, Kinzie," he said with a sneer.

Hugh stepped back. The big man had some guts. Hugh holstered his Colt.

Nettleton came forward. "What do you mean about not going through with the plan?" he demanded.

Hugh looked out into the quiet canyon. "Those horses and mules wouldn't get ten miles. We don't even know if there is a trail beyond this canyon. If you left here right now it would be daylight long before you got out of this canyon. The damned thing may go on for miles, every inch of it overlooked by the Mimbrenos. As for your so-called sortie. If you took every man you have here you'd all be dead long before you reached the 'camp' of the Mimbrenos, as Phillips called it. They haven't any camp with rows of tents and bivouac fires going. They're lying out in the brush in the darkness, listening to every night sound. You could walk right through the middle of the camp and never know it was there until knives came up from the very ground itself to gut you. If five of us went looking for those bastards in the dark, as was suggested here, none of us would come back, and if we did get a crack at them before they got us, we'd hardly make a dent in their forces. Then they'd be after the main party. They could outrun our horses afoot."

Clymer spat. "So? What do *you* suggest?"

Hugh shrugged. "It seems I'm the only one here without an idea."

Phillips wiped the blood from the corner of his mouth. "Perhaps one man might get through to the Rio Grande and bring back help."

Nettleton bobbed his head. "A capital thought, Mr. Phillips."

Clymer glanced at Hugh. "*Him*, I suppose?"

"You can volunteer," said Hugh dryly.

"Will you go?" asked Nettleton. He gripped Hugh by the arm.

"I could go. I *might* get through. But as for bringing back help, that's out of the question. There aren't enough men in the Department of New Mexico right now to defend the Rio Grande Valley. Canby certainly won't send troops into these mountains to get wiped out."

Clymer wet his thick lips. He glanced back at the dwelling where Marion Nettleton was. "Perhaps I could get through with one of the women."

Phillips touched the corner of his mouth. "I can do the same," he said.

Maurice Nettleton hesitated, as he always did. He looked at Hugh. "My wife," he said quietly. "I know she wouldn't go without me, but perhaps I can force her to." He looked hopefully at Hugh. "What do you think, Kinzie?"

"Go ahead," said Hugh. "Mr. Clymer is willing."

Nettleton tugged at his side whiskers. "I didn't have him in mind. You're the most skilled of us in this type of business. We can cover you until you're in the clear. Marion is not strong, but she has courage. Will you take her?"

"You mean you're sacrificing yourself to save your wife?" asked Hugh dryly.

"Yes."

"You seem to have forgotten something, Nettleton."

"So?"

"Katy Corse."

The sudden quiet that followed Hugh's words was suddenly broken by the splitting crash of a gun at the east end of the canyon. The report slammed back and forth between the canyon walls.

"An attack!" cried Nettleton. "Turn out the guard!"

Booted feet slammed on the terrace. Shadowy figures formed along the terrace wall. Matt Hastings buckled on his gunbelt. "Check your carbines! Check the caps on your revolving pistols!" he said. "Corporal Roswell!"

"Here!"

"Greer!"

"Here!"

"Pearce!"

There was no answer. Hastings looked up and down the shadowed terrace. "Pearce!" he called out angrily.

Willis appeared on the terrace.

"Stevens!" said Hastings.

"Yo!"

"Willis!"

"Here!"

Hastings shoved back his hat. "Where's Pearce?"

"Damned if I know, Sergeant." said Willis. He glanced up the canyon.

"Anyone see him?" asked Hastings.

There was no answer.

"That sonofabitch go over the hill?" asked Hastings.

"Couldn't blame him," said Willis.

"Shut up!"

The canyon was quiet again. Hugh padded behind the enlisted men and stopped at the far end of the terrace. He looked towards the great rock wall. The shot had come from somewhere near it.

Hastings came up behind Hugh. "What do you think?" he asked.

Hugh shrugged. "You find Pearce?"

"No."

They waited. Now and then one of the waiting men moved. One of them coughed. A carbine butt thudded against the terrace.

Hastings looked at Hugh. "You think it was him, Kinzie?"

Hugh rubbed his jaw. "The shot came from near that dead mule. There was silver on the mule. You think Pearce would want that silver enough to go up there?"

"He had larceny in his soul."

Hugh looked up at the sky, then down at the ground. "Wherever he is, his damned larceny took him there then."

"Maybe he's lying out there wounded."

Hugh looked along the mesa wall. There was a faint trail there, with a sheer wall rising up beside it to the mesa top.

"I can take a look-see along that," he said quietly. "I might be able to see down into the canyon from there."

"He ain't worth it," a dry voice said behind them.

"Shut up, Willis," said Hastings.

Willis grinned. "I'll go along with the scout," he said.

Hugh vaulted over the low wall and handed his carbine to Hastings. "You can see us from here. I'm not worried about them getting at us from the mesa side. But they can get up through that brush to below the trail. If they come at us, keep firing between us and them."

Willis leaned his carbine against the wall and loosened his Colt in its holster. "Shoot at anything what don't wear a hat, Sarge," he said.

Willis followed Hugh along the steep slope until they reached the trail. There was no sign of life. Silence ruled the canyon.

A hundred yards from the ruins, Hugh looked back over his shoulder. The face of the trooper was plain to see in the moonlight. There was something about Chandler Willis that didn't quite fit right with Hugh. He was a hard worker and usually willing. He did his duty, no more, no less. Yet he always seemed to be waiting for something.

Hugh paused at a place where a rock shoulder cast deep shadows against the mesa wall. The moon shone on the areas of sand and rock with a silvery light. The rocks and brush drew etched shadows behind them. There was no movement.

Willis scratched his corded throat. "Now what?"

Hugh studied the canyon floor. It looked as empty as a crater on the moon. Something warned him to go back. He had no particular liking for Dan Pearce.

"Let's go back," suggested Willis quietly.

"I thought you wanted to make a break from the party," Hugh said.

Willis half closed his eyes. "Now, scout," he said quietly, "you got no idea of making a break now."

Hugh looked down into the canyon,

trying to locate the place where the mule had died.

"You haven't, have you?" persisted Willis.

"No. But why did you come along with me?"

"I don't want nothing to happen to you, scout."

Hugh glanced at the secretive man beside him. "Stay here," he said. "Cover me until I'm out of sight in that brush clump near the big rock fall."

Willis nodded. He shifted his chew and spat. "Be careful, scout. I don't want nothin' to happen to you."

"Your concern touches my heart," said Hugh dryly.

He slipped along the trail, using every patch of concealment, until he was even with a thicket of brush which rested at one end of the great rock fall. He loosened his knife in its sheath and swiftly touched his Colt butt. Then he eased down the slope and into the brush, moving like a hunting panther.

He reached the first slope of the rock

fall, which had angled out from the canyon entrance. Sometime in the past, there had been another great rock fall, which had cascaded down the first slopes, leaving a transverse ridge of loose rock down the older slope. The mule had died just beyond the ridge.

Hugh's every nerve seemed to be sensitized. He could smell the pungent odour of the brush, still warm from the heat of the day, mingled with the sour smell of his sweat-soaked clothing. He stood absolutely still except for his eyes, which scanned the moonlit terrain ahead. Now and then his nostrils quivered as he drew in a sharp breath, trying to get a scent. Something puzzled him. The mule had been out there long enough to develop gasses. Sense of smell and hearing should have been warned by now, for dead things can whisper restlessly when cool night air contracts warm flesh.

Hugh got down on his knees and crawled forward slowly, feeling his way with his hands, settling loose rock and placing each knee carefully. Sweat worked down his body and he mentally cursed the scouring his hands and knees were taking from the sharp edges of rock.

He lay flat just before he reached the crest of the ridge. He listened, then crawled forward, easing into the shadow of a tilted slab of rock. He looked down the far slope. Then he knew why he hadn't got wind of the mule. He could see the moonlight on the big white bones. The carcass had been stripped for meat and guts, as cleanly as though buzzards had been at work. Apaches had a preference for sweet mule meat.

The moonlight shone dully on something else, beyond the ravaged carcass of the mule. Something like pools of water dappling the sandy earth. Hugh was puzzled until he remembered the silver service.

Where in the hell was Pearce? Maybe the burly New Yorker hadn't come out here at all. Maybe the gun had been shot at something else. Maybe . . . The thought trailed off in Hugh's mind. He slowly turned his head to look along the rock ridge, then down into the canyon, then up the steep northern wall, to follow along the rock which almost blocked the entrance. A Mescalero had once told him something he should have remembered: "White-Eyes hear shot. Run like hell to see what happen. Tinneh hear shot. No run to see. Stay tight in hiding place. Wait. Wait. Wait, until sure no one in ambush."

Hugh bellied down the slope in the shelter of the brush. He lay flat beside a large boulder. There was something ahead of him, dimly seen through the tangled brush. Something white. He inched forward on the warm earth until he could see what it was.

The body lay on its back, the thick mats of curly black hair in deep contrast to the whiteness of the skin. The skin looked unusually white compared to the mahogany brown of the big hands. The contorted face was yet another hue. Hugh looked away for a moment. The skull had been crushed and blood had coated the broad face in a dark mask. The bloody eyes stared unseeingly up at the moonlit sky.

Hugh inched back. Something else caught his eye. Dan Pearce clutched a beautifully formed silver creamer in his right hand.

Hugh did not hurry on his return trip, although the hounds of fear ran silently at his heels. He made his way carefully up the slope until he reached the place where Chandler Willis waited for him. There was no need to say anything to Willis. He knew.

They walked slowly back towards the cliff dwellings. They were almost to the crumbling wall when Willis spoke softly. "One down," he said. "Twelve to go. Who's next, scout?"

11

MATT HASTINGS marked it down in his little notebook. "Pearce, D. A., Pvt—from duty to deceased," he said. He wrote down the time and date.

"What's the A stand for?" asked Willis.

"Aloysius."

"Hell," said Willis. "No wonder he'd never tell me."

Isaiah Morton stood at the edge of the terrace with his lean hands clasped together. "Therefore thus saith the Lord of hosts, the God of Israel; Behold, I will feed them, even this people, with wormwood, and give them water of gall to drink."

"There he goes again," said Willis.

Isaiah Morton raised his voice. "I will scatter them also among the heathen, whom neither they nor their fathers have

160

known: and I will send a sword after them, till I have consumed them."

The men looked at each other with wide eyes. Hastings closed his notebook. "Morton," he said quietly, "this J Company wasn't issued a chaplain, and if it had been, I'd tell him to say something cheerful from the Good Book. Any more of that stuff out of you and I'll heave you over the wall so you can go amongst those heathen, whom neither us nor our fathers have known. *Comprende*?"

Morton's eyes seemed to shine through the darkness. He stalked off down the terrace. "They shall have eyes and they shall not see not," he intoned. "They shall have ears and they shall hear not."

"Makes my skin crawl," said Hastings. "The man is a Jonah."

They could hear the horses and mules plainly. Stevens looked towards them. "By God, Sarge," he said hoarsely, "they're really suffering. I can't listen to 'em much longer."

Hastings opened his mouth to curse Stevens, and then he shut it. They were all horsemen. None of them liked the idea of letting the horses suffer. Hastings looked at Hugh. Hugh raised his head and drew a forefinger across his lean throat.

Hastings nodded. "I'll tell the captain," he said.

"Tell him what, Sarge?" demanded Stevens.

"None of your damned business."

Stevens stepped forward and dropped his carbine across his left forearm. "You mean you're going to kill off those horses?"

Hastings lowered his right hand to his Colt butt. "Not all of them. We've got three extras now. Pearce's mount and the two pack mules. God knows there isn't enough water for those that will be left, but we'll have to sweat out a day or two more before we figure out what to do with them."

Stevens cocked his carbine. "You're not going to kill any of them," he said quietly. "Let them go. They'll take care of themselves."

Hastings eyed the trooper. "Look, jaybird," he said, "we're out of food. I don't like horse or mule meat but I'll be damned if I'm going to starve as long as I can get some of it. Now you let down the hammer of that carbine and get to your post before I show you the hard way who's first soldier around here."

Stevens stood there for half a minute, then he eased down his carbine hammer and walked slowly towards the west end of the terrace.

"The sonofabitch actually thinks more of them damned animals being kept alive than he does of us eating," said Matt Hastings.

"Who'll slaughter them?" asked Hugh.

Hastings whirled. "Not me!"

"Then who?"

"You!"

Hugh shook his head. "I killed my best horse two years ago when Comanches had me cut off from the column. Dropped him with a shot between the eyes to use him so I could fort up in a buffalo wallow.

163

I can still remember how he looked just before he got the bullet."

Hastings pulled at his lip. "Yeah, yeah."

The five of them stood there in the dimness: Hugh, Hastings, Roswell, Willis and Greer. Hastings cleared his throat. "We can draw straws," he said.

"No need," said Harry Roswell. "I'll do it."

The other four looked quickly at Roswell. Greer wet his thin lips, then turned and walked away. Willis shoved back his hat, shrugged, and then sauntered towards the east end of the terrace.

"Both mules and one of the horses," said Roswell. "Which horse?"

Hastings shrugged. "Pick out the worst of the lot." He grinned as he looked towards the shadowy line of animals tethered at the west end of the terrace. "Stevens's," he said.

Roswell leaned his carbine against the wall and reached for his Colt. Hugh placed a hand on Roswell's wrist. "Use the knife." he said. "We can't spare ammunition. Besides . . . we don't want to arouse the Apaches."

Roswell nodded. He wet his lips. Hugh drew out his heavy sheath knife and handed it to the noncom. Roswell hefted it, then walked towards the animals.

"Lead them away one at a time from the others!" called out Hugh. "If the rest of them smell the blood they'll get excited."

Roswell nodded without turning. "I couldn't do it," said Greer from the shadows.

"You can't do anything," said Hastings.

"Maybe the officers won't like it," said Greer.

Hastings spat. "There'll be a helluva lot more they won't like before we get out of this hell-hole."

Roswell was holding the first horse by the bridle reins now. Somebody spoke to him.

"Whose horse is that?" asked Hugh suddenly.

Hastings stared. "Stevens's," he said.

Hugh started forward. "The damned fool should have known better."

Roswell was dragging at the bridle reins of Stevens's bay. Suddenly there was a sharp cry from Stevens. He hit Roswell with the butt of his carbine. The noncom staggered towards the terrace wall, dropping the knife. Stevens was up on his bay. He shrieked like a Comanche and drove the excited bay against the horse next in line. The horses and mules jerked at their tethers. One by one they broke loose, neighing sharply and clashing their hoofs against the floor of the terrace.

Stevens whooped. He slapped the nearest rumps with his hat. A horse leaped the terrace wall and crashed down the slope. Roswell screamed as the frenzied animals surged towards him. He was driven against the wall. Rocks crumbled as the hoofs struck sparks from them. Then the whole mass of them were over the wall and floundering down the slope in an uproar that echoed and re-echoed through the canyon. Dust rose in a pall and swept back towards the cliff dwellings.

Hugh raced towards Roswell. He could see Stevens behind the stampeding animals, waving his hat and screaming wildly. The group of horses and mules reached the bottom of the slope and crashed through a dense thicket. Then they were in the clear, racing towards the east end of the canyon with a steady drumming of hoofs.

Nettleton ran alongside Hugh. "What happened?"

Hugh didn't answer. He crouched beside Roswell. The noncom was unconscious. Blood stained his face and ran from the corner of his mouth. One arm hung at an awkward angle. A bubbling sound came from his throat as he breathed.

The bitter smell of dust hung in the night air. The drumming of the hoofs was dying away when the flat crack of a rifle carried to those who stood on the terrace.

"I wonder what he thought he was doing?" asked Katy Corse.

"He's loco," said Chandler Willis.

Hugh wiped the blood from Roswell's face. "He's in a bad way. Help me get him into one of the rooms."

Willis and Hastings helped Hugh with the injured man. Katy Corse came into the room after they lowered Roswell on to his blanket. "Get some cloth for bandages," said Hugh over his shoulder.

Katy bent forward and pulled up her skirt. She looked at the torn and dirty petticoat she wore. "It won't help him any to put cloth like this against his wounds."

Hugh wiped the blood from Roswell's chin and neck. "Ask Mrs. Nettleton for some of her things. She's got a packful of them."

Katy nodded. She left the room. Hastings looked down at Roswell. "What do you think, Kinzie?" he asked softly.

Hugh stood up. "He's all smashed up inside."

Hastings shook his head. "I never thought he'd take me serious when I told him to kill Stevens's horse."

Willis leaned against the wall. "You knew damned well he always did what he was told, Sarge."

Hastings looked up. "Yeah. Yeah."

Abel Clymer burst into the room. "Hastings!" he snapped. "We've got to get those horses back at once."

Far down the canyon another shot cracked faintly, like a faggot snapping in the fireplace.

"If the lieutenant will tell me how," he said coolly, "I'll be glad to try."

Clymer looked from one to the other of the three men standing in front of him. "Who's responsible for that stampede?"

"If we told you, what would you do, Clymer?" asked Hugh. "Court-martial him?"

"We're trapped for sure now!" snapped Clymer.

Hugh studied the blustering officer. "You've been trapped ever since you left the Fort McLane trail and came up into these mountains."

There was doubt in Clymer's eyes now.

He looked down at Roswell. "How badly is he hurt?"

"He's all smashed up inside, Mr. Clymer," said Hastings.

"You think he'll live?"

Hastings stared at the big officer. "I hope so, sir!"

Clymer looked about the dim room. "Where's Greer?"

"Somewhere outside."

Clymer turned and left the room.

Hastings eased Roswell's head back on to a fold of the blanket. "Clymer sounded almost like he wanted Roswell to die . . . I wonder why?"

"I suppose he figures Roswell will be nothing but a burden now," Hugh said.

Katy Corse came in, carrying a petticoat over her arm. "Get some water, Willis," she said.

Willis looked at Hugh. Hugh nodded. Willis left the room. Hastings took a stub of candle from his pocket and lit it, placing it in a wall niche. The flickering yellow light seemed to accentuate the ghastly pallor of Roswell's face. Katy handed the petticoat to Hastings. "Rip it up," she said.

Hastings whistled as he felt the fine material. "My God, but our cat had a fine long tail, Katy. What'd she say when you asked for it?"

Katy brushed back her hair. "I didn't ask her. If I had, and she'd refused me, I would have taken it any way."

Hugh walked outside. Abel Clymer was part-way down the slope, staring off to the west as though he could penetrate the gigantic shoulder of rock which blocked off the mysteries of the western part of the canyon.

Darrell Phillips came up behind Hugh. "I wish he'd take a walk up that canyon," he said softly.

Hugh looked quickly at the officer. "We're getting short-handed," he said. "First Pearce. Then Stevens and Roswell. Morton is useless and Greer isn't much better."

Phillips waved a hand. "All the same, I wish to God he'd walk into an Apache trap."

"Who's on guard?"

"I don't know."

"Damn it!" Hugh turned on a heel and walked towards the watch-tower. He turned quickly into the narrow passageway. There was a sudden movement in the darkness. Boots grated against rock. Then something smashed and tinkled against the rock wall. The pungent odour of strong liquor flowed towards Hugh. He darted forward but whoever had dropped the bottle was gone in the darkness of the passageway which led behind the cliff dwellings.

Hugh returned to the terrace. Hastings and Willis were with Roswell and Katy. Nettleton was with his wife. Phillips was standing at the far end of the terrace looking down into the canyon. Abel Clymer was part way down the slope, looking in the direction the horses and mules had gone. Hugh nodded. He walked to the passageway which led back to the triangular passageway behind the dwellings. There was a furtive movement in the darkness. Hugh reached out with a big hand and clamped it on Greer's shirt collar. He drew the squirming little man towards him.

Greer struck at Hugh. Hugh shook him a little. Greer bared his yellowish teeth. "You've got no right to treat me like this!"

Hugh thrust his face close to Greer's. "You drunken little bastard! Where did you get the stuff?"

Greer drew back. "Down in one of those round rooms below the terrace."

Hugh shoved the little orderly back against the wall. "There was a time when nothing short of a jab in the rump from Satan's pitchfork would have made you go down there."

Greer shakily held out a hand. "Don't tell the captain," he pleaded.

"Have you got another bottle?"

"No!"

Hugh swiftly passed his hands over the little man's body. Greer was clean. Hugh thrust a big finger under Greer's nose as though he was admonishing a little child. "I get one whiff of liquor from you,

Greer, and I'll break your Goddamned neck like a matchstick. *Comprende?*"

Greer straightened up. He stroke his skinny neck. "A man has to have something around here to keep up his courage."

"You never had any in the first place."

"Go to hell, Kinzie!"

Hugh stepped back. "Get your carbine. Get out on that terrace and keep your eyes peeled."

Greer watched Hugh walk back towards the terrace. The little orderly scurried back into the triangular passageway. He reached up into a cleft and gripped a bottle. Swiftly, with shaking hands, he drew out the cork. He tipped up the bottle and let the flaming liquor flow down his open throat. He gulped as though he were tasting mother's milk, then took down the bottle, corked it and cached it. He wiped his mouth with the back of his dirty hand and grinned in the darkness. "Go to hell, Kinzie," he said softly.

Hugh walked to the ladder which

protruded from one of the openings in the terrace floor. He eased his way down it until his feet hit the floor. He took out a candle stub and lit it, placing it on one of the low shelves which encircled the room. Part of the contents of the mule packs had been stored in the room. Hugh lifted some of the articles with a boot toe, shaking his head as he did so. Boxes of clothing, hat boxes, bags of odds and ends and several tablecloths. There was no liquor amongst the things.

Something moved up on the terrace. Hugh blew out the candle and climbed the ladder. Greer was at the west end of the terrace, looking down into the canyon. There was no one else on the terrace. Hugh heard Harry Roswell groan in deep-seated agony. He walked to the next underground opening and went down the rickety ladder. He relit the candle and looked about the room. There were some rawhide panniers lying to one side. Hugh knelt beside them and opened the first of them. The necks of bottles showed through the straw packing.

The ladder creaked. Hugh turned. A pair of heavy legs showed coming down through the opening. Hugh squatted on his heels. Abel Clymer's broad shoulders came down through the opening. He eyed Hugh suspiciously. "What are you doing down here?" he demanded.

Hugh looked down at the liquor pannier. "Roswell might need some of this before he's through," he said.

Clymer stood on the ladder, breathing heavily. His eyes were slitted. "That's Nettleton's property," he said.

Hugh stood up. "All the same, Roswell is in bad shape. If it helps to ease his pain he can drink the whole damned load."

Clymer stepped on to the gritty floor and raised his head. "I said it was Nettleton's property."

Hugh leaned back against one of the low pilasters which held up the cribbed log roof. "How is it you're suddenly so concerned about Nettleton's property?" he asked softly.

Clymer flushed. "What do you mean?"

Hugh looked up at the ceiling. "Nothing."

Clymer didn't quite know what to do. Kinzie did not respect his bars and he certainly wasn't afraid. "You mean Mrs. Nettleton?" he blurted out at last.

Hugh looked surprised. "Why, *Abel!*"

Clymer spat to one side. "She's a lady," he said. "As an officer and a gentleman it's part of my duty to see that she's safely escorted to Santa Fe."

"Bravo!" said Hugh dryly.

Clymer thrust out a big hand, stabbing the forefinger towards Hugh's face. "You're nothing but a God-damned civilian scout. I don't like your attitude and I don't like you. Now get up there and take care of your job."

Hugh reached down and took a bottle from the pannier. He read the label. "This will do for a starter," he said. He walked past the big man and stopped at the bottom of the ladder. He looked back over his shoulder. "You're nothing but a God-damned army officer. I don't like your attitude and I don't like you. I'll take care of my job, Clymer, and I'm wondering if you can take care of yours before we get out of this mess."

Hugh climbed the ladder. He walked over to the room where Harry Roswell lay in agony. He handed the bottle to Katy. Matt Hastings eyed it. Chandler Willis wet his thin lips. Katy looked at the bottle. "Do you think he can take it?" she asked.

Hugh shoved back his hat. Sweat dewed Roswell's ghostly face in great clear beads. "There isn't anything else," he said.

"How long will he last?"

"*Quien sabe?*"

Roswell opened his eyes. "I was only doing my duty," he said clearly.

"Sure. Sure," said Hastings. He wiped the sweat from Roswell's face.

Roswell stared up at the ceiling. "I always did my duty," he said. "Jonas had no right to do that. He should be court-martialled for what he did."

"Sure," said Hastings. He glanced at the bottle. "How does it feel, Harry?"

Roswell closed his eyes. "Bad. I'm all busted up inside, Sergeant."

Katy handed Hastings the bottle. The first sergeant worked the wire and wrapping from the cork and pulled it out. He poured some of the liquor into a tin cup and gently lifted Roswell's head and shoulders. The injured man sipped at the liquor. Then he gulped at it.

Hugh tapped Chandler Willis's shoulder. "Get outside," he said. "Greer is on guard and I don't trust him."

Willis grinned. "And you trust *me*, Kinzie? How nice!" He picked up his carbine and walked outside.

Hastings looked up at Hugh. "What's bothering him?"

"Who knows?"

"He thinking of pulling foot out of here?"

"Who isn't?"

Hastings stood up. "I'll break his God-damned back if he tries."

"If you catch him, Matt. Besides, he won't try it alone."

"Meaning?"

"He might have tried it with Pearce. He wants me to make a break with him."

Hastings came close to Hugh. "Don't try, Kinzie," he said. "I've seen J Company outfits, but this is the worst yet. We've lost three men now. The only way any of us will get out of here alive is by all of us sticking together. I think you could make it alone . . . but you won't."

"How so?"

"You've got a certain sense of honour."

"That all?"

The hard eyes bored into Hugh's. "I'll kill any man, officer, enlisted man or civilian who tries to make the break alone."

Hugh shrugged. He walked to the door. "Katy," he said, "I'll have Mrs. Nettleton come in after a while to relieve you."

Katy brushed back her dark hair. Then she laughed. "Hugh, there are times

180

when you reveal an unconscious sense of ridiculous humour."

"She'll be here," said Hugh. He walked out on the terrace.

Matt Hastings squatted beside Katy. "*That*, I'll have to see," he said.

12

MARION NETTLETON smiled as Hugh came into the room she shared with her husband. Maurice Nettleton looked up. "How is Roswell?" he asked.

"Not good."

Nettleton bit his lip. He tugged at his sideburns. "We can't afford to lose another man, Kinzie."

"I took the liberty of appropriating one of your bottles of liquor for him. To ease the pain."

"Quite all right. Poor fellow. Is there anything else we can do for him?"

"Yes. Miss Corse is taking care of him now. I'd like Mrs. Nettleton to relieve her off and on during the night."

Nettleton stood up. "Absolutely not! Mrs. Nettleton is far too delicate of constitution for such work."

Marion Nettleton looked at her

husband. "Why, Maurice!" she said quickly. "I'll be more than glad to help. I'm a soldier's wife. I must learn to do this type of work."

Maurice Nettleton stared at his wife. There were times when he wondered about her. She had once said she'd never have children because of the pain and mess involved. It had struck sharply home to him and he had never forgotten it. Now here she was volunteering to attend a badly smashed sick man who hadn't had a bath in several weeks. It was beyond Maurice Nettleton to figure her out.

Marion looked at Hugh. "What time do you want me there?"

"In about an hour. Katy will spend most of the night with him, but she must have some sleep. You can work it out with her."

She smiled. "I'm sure we will."

Hugh left the room. He glanced back at it. He had expected something quite different from Marion Nettleton. No wonder she had that poor bastard of a husband under her pretty thumb.

Myron Greer looked out of the tower window. The moon bathed the canyon in pure silver light. The liquor was bubbling gently inside him. He grinned as he leaned on the sill of the window. That God-damned Hugh Kinzie wasn't all he seemed to be.

Greer looked up the terrace. Kinzie was at the far end with Darrell Phillips. Greer slid down to the next floor of the tower and then down into the first floor. He stood there in the darkness, listening like a prowling coyote. He was too damned clever for Kinzie to outmanoeuvre. Greer leaned his carbine against the wall and eased his way into the passage. From up above him he could hear the occasional dripping of water. Myron Greer didn't need food nor water when he had a bottle cached away.

He worked his way down the cluttered passageway at the rear of the dwellings, fumbled in the niche for his treasure, then drew the bottle down to his lips. He drank sparingly and replaced the bottle. He walked partway back to his post, feeling the liquor flame within him. Maybe he'd better have another snort. He might not be able to leave his post again. He hurried back to the niche. He got the bottle and uncorked it, then stopped short. Something had moved down the passageway towards the east end of the dwellings. He corked the bottle and raised it towards the niche. He could see the man fairly well now. It was Abel Clymer. No one else would fill the passageway as the big officer did.

Abel Clymer was fumbling about in a pile of fallen rocks and debris. He did not look towards Myron Greer. Greer took the cork from the bottle and drank deeply. Craftily, he hid the bottle in another place. Then he eased his way back towards his post, stopping at the corner of the tower to watch Clymer. Clymer was concentrating on something. Then he replaced whatever he had in his hands in the hole and covered it with

185

rocks and debris. Greer faded around the corner and climbed up to his post. His head was swimming a little with the exertion, and his feet stumbled on the notches of the chicken ladder. He drew himself up into the top room of the tower and leaned for a time against the wall. The room seemed to sway and lift a little as though it were floating on water.

The moon was at its highest. Jonas Stevens lay on his face, clawed fingers buried to the second joints in the bloody sand. He looked curiously flattened. He had seen the Apache before he had fired. Jonas had spurred his bay to get ahead of the stampeding horses and mules and had succeeded just in time to be slammed from his saddle by the impact of a heavy rifle ball. The horses and mules had done the rest. The horses and mules Jonas Stevens had been trying to save.

Harry Roswell opened his eyes and

looked up into the oval face of Marion Nettleton. "Is it time for First Call?" he asked.

"No," she said quietly.

He closed his eyes. "I thought I heard the trumpet." He coughed harshly.

She raised his shoulders and head. The sour smell of the man sickened her. She wondered how Katy Corse had been able to spend the last two hours sitting here beside the dying man. She lowered the trooper and wiped his face with a damp cloth. His breath was sour and thick with liquor fumes. Drying blood caked his lips. His breathing seemed to bubble deep in his chest. Sweat broke out on his pallid forehead.

Marion reached over and pinched out the candle. The moonlight streamed in through the small windows. A cold finger of fear seemed to trace the length of her spine, almost as though Death had entered the room the instant she had put out the candle, and had touched her to let her know he was there waiting the end too.

Darrell Phillips was standing his guard at the east end of the terrace. Death had struck hard three times within the past few hours. Dan Pearce had died out on the sands. Jonas Stevens had died somewhere down the canyon. Harry Roswell was fencing with Death in a losing battle. There was a cold loneliness in Darrell Phillips. There was a finality about the way things were happening. The course of events was shaping towards an ending which would, in all probability, find Darrell Phillips cold in death. He couldn't face it alone. He had to have Katy Corse beside him, so that her feminine strength would fill in the gap in his own strength, and the two of them together could face the end.

Abel Clymer leaned against a wall watching Hugh Kinzie. That damned scout had his nose into everything. Abel wondered if Kinzie had gone down into the underground room solely to find liquor for Roswell. Kinzie was always prowling around like a damned lean cat.

Kinzie knew how Abel felt about Marion Nettleton. Kinzie was always so damned sure of himself. That was one reason Abel had to take it easy. There was no one in the party who could serve Able Clymer as Hugh Kinzie could. The two of them might get out of this death trap and could take Marion Nettleton along to boot. Kinzie could be gotten rid of later when safety was in sight. Sweat broke out on Clymer's body. His hands shook in expectation. With Marion Nettleton and the stake he had cached away he'd be the biggest hero west of the Mississippi.

Clymer wet his lips. There were four men who had been with him when he had found Winston's body. Corporal Roswell, Privates Pearce, Willis and Stevens. Roswell was dying. Pearce was dead, and Stevens probably was, too. That left that slit-eyed bastard Willis to be reckoned with. He was secretive and sly. How much did he know?

Abel Clymer faded into the darkness as Hugh Kinzie walked slowly along the terrace, looking out into the mysterious moonlit canyon. A coyote howled softly from the top of the far wall.

Isaiah Morton pressed his thin hands against his burning eyes. There was a fire deep in his soul which seemed to gain in intensity as the days went on. There was no hunger in him and very little thirst, but his desire to carry the word of God to the heathens who held the party trapped, gained in intensity even as the insatiable flame which raged within him.

"Oh, my God, why dost thou persecute me?" he whispered. He laced his thin fingers together and pushed his hands downward as he raised his head and eyes upward. He shivered a little in his ecstasy of desire. "I will bring them truth, and the truth shall set them free. I shall make them walk as children of the light."

Hugh Kinzie padded along the terrace carrying the liquor panniers. He did not see the eyes that watched him from the tower. Hugh bent his head to enter the low doorway of the room where Harry Roswell was dying. "How is he?" he asked Marion.

She wearily brushed back a wisp of damp hair. "Asleep," she said.

"*Bueno!*" Hugh placed the panniers in a corner.

She eyed the panniers. "You don't think he'll need all that?"

"No. But it's safer here."

"Why?"

Hugh squatted beside her and felt for his tobacco pouch. "The food is almost gone. We've lost two men and will lose another before long. Nerves are getting frayed. At times like this men will turn to liquor for Dutch courage."

"A courage that quickly lets them down."

"Yes. May I smoke?"

She nodded. "If I may have one too."

She studied him as he rolled her a cigarette. "You're not surprised?"

He shook his head. "I've spent too

much time along the border to think twice about women smoking." He placed the cigarette between her full lips and lit it with a lucifer. The spurt of flame lit up her oval face. He blew out the match without taking his eyes from her.

She looked away. "You didn't make one of them for yourself," she said.

He jerked his head. "Oh!"

She watched his big fingers as they deftly rolled the cylinder of tobacco. "You seem to do everything well."

He placed the cigarette in his mouth and lit it. "Everything?"

"Everything I've seen you do, that is."

"That's better."

They smoked without speaking. Hugh looked at Harry Roswell. His face had undergone a subtle change; it seemed longer and sunken. It was as though the skull was trying to come through the flesh.

"Do you think there is a chance?" she asked.

"No."

"I didn't think you'd give up easily."

He glanced quickly at her. "Me? I'm not giving up. I thought you were talking about Harry."

"Well?"

He sat down with his back against the wall. "Some of us might make it to the Rio Grande."

She shivered a little despite herself. There was a fatalism in him she had not expected. But this was a man who could be depended upon.

Hugh inspected his cigarette. "My job is to get you to safety, Mrs. Nettleton."

She was startled. It was almost as though he had read her mind.

Hugh stood up. "I'll admit things look black, but it could be worse. We haven't been attacked in here. We have a little water."

She ground out her cigarette. "No horses. A handful of men, half of whom are useless encumbrances."

He shrugged. "I said some of us wouldn't make it."

"But you will?"

"Yes."

She stood up suddenly, standing so close to him her full breasts touched his shirt. "You once told me it was a fifty-fifty chance. Maybe less. You also promised me that you would stay close to me on the trail. Is that promise still good?" She placed her slim hands on his shoulders and looked up into his eyes. Her own promise was in her eyes. She knew how to use her weapons.

Hugh slid an arm about her waist and crushed her to him, feeling her breath on his face. She shivered a little as he bent his face close to hers. "Don't you think this is a hell of a place for dallying?" he asked softly. "With a dying man at our feet and your husband not fifty feet away?"

Her face flushed and then went taut. She bit her lip as she realized he was making a fool out of her. She struggled to break free. Suddenly he released her. She raised her hands to rake his face to bloody ribbons, but he was too fast for her. He kissed her so hard he bruised her lips and his whiskers scored her delicate skin. Then he shoved her back and walked to the door. He looked back at her.

"Take good care of Harry," he said quietly.

"Damn you!"

He grinned. "Remember you're a lady," he said with a strong hint of laughter in his voice.

She hurled a cup at the wall as he vanished from her sight . . .

Abel Clymer pressed his big body flat against the wall as Hugh Kinzie padded past. Clymer's thick lips drew back as he looked at the broad back of the scout. Clymer rested a hand on the butt of his revolving pistol. He had overheard them talking in the dwelling. He withdrew his hand. Let them talk. Both of them were part of his plan, and he wasn't part of theirs. Abel Clymer could play a waiting game. His time would come . . .

A coyote howled softly up the canyon. A night bird chirped from the brush. Harry Roswell opened his eyes and looked up at Marion Nettleton. "I

wish . . ." he said thickly. "I wish . . ."
His voice faded away. His breathing
stopped but his eyes were wide in his
head.

Marion Nettleton stared down at the
dead man. Then her control broke. She
screamed, and screamed again, awakening
the canyon echoes.

13

THEY buried Harry Roswell behind a crumbling wall in the debris from a fallen roof. There was no marker on the grave. No one would ever come here to find his grave, Hugh thought as he watched Chandler Willis and Matt Hastings finish the burial.

Hastings looked up at Hugh. "Where's Greer?"

"He was on guard."

"He isn't there now."

"Sleeping somewhere, then."

Hastings nodded. He took out his little notebook and marked it down. "Roswell, H. L., Corp.—from duty to deceased."

"What's the 'L' stand for?" asked Willis as he wiped the sweat from his lean face.

"Lemuel."

Isaiah Morton clasped his thin hands together and looked down at the unmarked grave. "Gone from this earth to his reward in Heaven," he said. "Our loss is Heaven's gain."

"That sonofabitch Stevens is responsible for this," said Matt Hastings.

"You mark Stevens down in your little book, Matt?" asked Hugh.

"Yes."

"How did you mark it?"

Hastings looked up. "Absent without leave. How else?"

"My God," said Hugh. "Always the first soldier."

"Our band of lost sheep gets smaller every day," said Morton. He bowed his head. "The Lord is my shepherd."

"Gives me the creeps," said Willis.

The mid-morning sun was beating down into the quiet canyon. The heat was soaking into the cliff dwellings. There wasn't a breath of wind to bring relief.

"You'd think them officers would have come," said Willis.

Hugh nodded. The signs were plain. Everyone was thinking of himself now, and that included Marion Nettleton.

Willis opened up his shirt and scratched his lean belly. "Any mess?" he asked Hastings.

"Nothing."

"This ain't the army any more. A man could leave right now if he had a mind to."

Hastings closed his book and stowed it away in his pocket. "Yeah," he said quietly. "Except for two things."

Willis spat leisurely. "What's to stop a man?"

Hastings held up two dirty fingers. "One," he said softly, "the Apaches. Two, me."

Willis yawned. He straightened up and then he walked down the pile of debris and into the triangular passageway.

"He's right," said Hugh.

Hastings turned quickly. "What do you mean?"

"It isn't the army any more, Matt. Each to his own from now on."

Hastings wiped the sweat from his face. "Go ahead, Kinzie. I won't try to stop you."

Hugh slid down the crumbling pile of debris. "I'll try to get some game," he said over his shoulder.

Morton was praying. Hastings eyed the cadaverous preacher. "Any way you can get some of that manna from Heaven?" he asked.

Morton did not answer.

"How about the miracle of the loaves and fishes?" asked Hastings.

Morton did not move. Hastings shrugged and left the room.

The strays came drifting down the canyon about noon. Five of them. All horses. It was Darrell Phillips who saw them first. "Look!" he called out in a cracked voice.

The others, with the exception of Myron Greer, ran out of the rooms where they had been trying to avoid the heat. They crouched behind the low terrace wall and looked at the horses.

"They've had water," said Hastings.

"They've had grass," said Willis.

The men looked at each other. Abel Clymer rested big paws on the top of the wall. "I'll give any man fifty dollars who'll bring in one of those horses."

There was a moment's silence and then Chandler Willis laughed dryly.

Hugh Kinzie eyed the far wall of the canyon. There was no sign of life. Whoever was directing the cruel game was a genius. He had timed it just right. Morale and unity were beginning to show great cracks throughout the little besieged party of White-eyes.

"A hundred dollars," said Abel Clymer.

"Shut up," said Hugh.

The strays drifted slowly into the shade of a great shoulder of rock. So near and yet so far. But it was worth far more than a hundred dollars to cross that stretch of baking rock and sand. It was worth a man's life.

By mid-afternoon the heat was intense. There was no trace yet of wind in the lifeless air. Nothing moved, not even the strays, who stood with bent heads in the hot shadow of the rock shoulder.

Matt Hastings ran his tongue over his cracked lips. He looked at Hugh. "What do you think?" he asked.

"Don't try it, Matt."

"Maybe after dark?"

"They have ears like dogs."

"Yeah."

Minutes ticked past. Hastings slid his carbine forward and checked the cap. He placed his hand on his pistol butt. He looked at Hugh from out of slitted eyes.

Hugh held up a thumb and looked up from beneath the brim of his hat. A buzzard floated high overhead in the windless air like a scrap of charred paper. The shadow flitted across the yellowish floor of the canyon.

Matt Hastings rested his head on his forearms. "Bad luck," he said.

The steady pounding of Hugh's heart seemed to be like the swinging pendulum of a clock marking the slow passage of time. Sweat trickled greasily down his body and he realized it had been quite some time since he had bathed. He touched his face. The bristles were thick upon his jaws.

Hastings suddenly laughed. It sounded so strange to Hugh that he raised his head to stare at the big first sergeant. Maybe he was cracking up. Hastings' sunburned face was set in a grin, but there was no mirth in his eyes.

"What's the joke?" asked Hugh.

Hastings tenderly touched his cracked lips, aggravated by the strain of his wide grin. "I was thinking of old Dobe-gusndi-he. He was a sub-chief of the White Mountain Apaches. Never could catch the wily old bastard. Finally one of his warriors sold him out for a sack of bullets, a butcher knife and a bottle of red-eye. We closed in on him near Escudilla Mountain. Run him to earth in a box canyon just like this. He had no water. No food. Damned little powder and ball." Hastings rested his head wearily on his forearms.

"So?"

Hastings looked up. He wiped the sweat from his eyes. "We had him . . .

lock, stock and barrel. But he wouldn't surrender. Not that old devil. But we got him."

"How?"

"Wasn't no sense in charging in on him. He was like a cornered rat. Mr. Ballard was our CO—a good soldier and a mathematician. He studies the lay of the land. The Apaches was holed up under a big cave just like this one we're under. Open ground in front—no cover at all. No way to get at them from either side or from the top. But we got 'em. All of 'em."

"Keep talking. It kills the monotony."

"Yeah. Well, as I said, Ballard was a mathematician. He looks at the slope of the cave roof, does some figuring. Says something about the angle of rebound being the same as the angle of incidence. Whatever that meant at the time I didn't know, but I learned damned soon. Ballard tells us to aim at the cave ceiling. We fired volleys until the barrels were misty with heat. At first we heard screams. Then groans. Then nothing. Ballard stands up like he was on parade and walks right into that God-damned cave like there was nobody there."

"So?"

Hastings looked steadily at Hugh. "Those slugs had bounced down from the roof right into those Apaches behind the boulders. It was awful! The slugs had keyholed into them. There was pieces of skull with hair still on them scattered all over. Not one of them poor bastards was alive. It looked like we had given them a dose of canister or grape at pointblank range from a mountain howitzer. But we didn't lose a man."

Hugh felt a little sick.

Hastings closed his eyes. "Ballard got a promotion. Later he was ordered to West Point to teach mathematics."

"It figures."

Hastings looked up at the reddish rock which formed the roof of the cave over the dwellings. "That place was just like this."

Hugh leaned back against the terrace

wall. "I've been trying to figure out what Dobe-gusndi-he means."

Hastings laughed dryly. "That's the joke. It means invulnerable."

"Stop," said Hugh. "You're killing me."

Hastings stared at Hugh for a minute, then burst into cackling laughter. "That's one thing I've always liked about you, Kinzie," he said. "You've got the dryest damned sense of humour."

Hugh stood up and looked back at the heat-soaked dwellings. "Speaking of dryness," he said quietly. "I'm going to take a look-see for Greer."

"I hope that sonofabitch is dead. He never was a soldier and never will be."

"We might need him before we get out of here."

"*Him?*" Hastings spat dryly. "He's nothing but a burden. Like that psalm-singing bastard Morton."

Hugh shrugged. "We'll have to do something before long, Matt."

Hastings rubbed his jaw. "Yeah. But what?"

"*Na-tse-kes*."

"What in the hell is that?"

Hugh looked out at the canyon, silent and foreboding under the brilliant sun. "One thought at a time, over and over again in the mind, exclusive of all others."

"Sometimes I think you're part Injun."

"One thought at a time: how to get out of here . . . *alive*." Hugh walked towards the dwellings.

Hastings rubbed the stock of his gun and looked across at the far wall of the canyon. "Yeah," he said softly. "Yeah. I know what you mean, hombre."

Hugh looked along the line of crumbling buildings. Thirteen people had come there for sanctuary. Three of them were dead. The sanctuary had become a prison and the sentence for each of the remaining ten people there was death.

14

MYRON GREER lay in the hiding place he had found. There he was safe from the prying eyes of the others in the party. His liquor supply had run out and he had been looking for more when he had found his hiding-place. A roof had collapsed at one side, forming a triangular-shaped pocket between the floor and the wall. Greer had crawled inside and had carefully arranged rocks to conceal the entrance. It was stifling hot. His clothing was soggy with sweat and irritated his itching skin. Now and then the white worms seemed to moil and heave in his gut. A mallet thudded steadily at the base of his skull, and opening his eyes, even in the semi-darkness, seemed to send a lance of burning pain deep into his skull.

There was a searing thirst in Myron Greer's throat and a more terrible thirst in his soul. He rested his head against the gritty earthen floor of the dwelling. It had always been the same with him. He had never quite fitted anywhere. As a child he had been unwanted, even by his playmates, because of his ungainliness and lack of skill even in the simplest sports and games. His father had been a big, powerful man with a huge bump of self-ego and a determination to push himself to the top. Myron's mother had protected and defended him, encouraging him with his books and studies. He had been better than average in that, in any case.

In college he had found out that the bottle is a good prop for a man who is never sure of himself. It had carried him through four years. By the end of that time he had a degree and a perpetual thirst which kept him from holding a job for more than a month or two. He was all right until he got his wages, then the glass spurs—whisky glasses—would take over, and Myron Greer would get on a two- or a three-day drunk, lose his job, and suffer for a week with the after-effects of the rotgut. Gradually he had managed to stay drunk most of the time to escape a hangover and the more feared sieges of remorse.

He had drifted West and while drunk he had enlisted, to fill out a recruiting sergeant's quota for the month and to prove to a derisive group of fellow drunks and giggling hurdy-gurdy girls that Myron Greer really was a man.

Greer gently beat his throbbing head on the floor. He was sicker than he had ever been on coming out of a bout with John Barleycorn. The only thing that would help was more of the same. Hugh Kinzie had taken the liquor from the rooms below the terrace and had been keeping an eye on that marvellous store of liquid joy.

Suddenly he remembered seeing that big sonofabitch Clymer pawing around in a pile of debris the night before. Greer sat up suddenly and smashed his head against one of the ancient roof beams. He winced. Then he licked his dry cracked lips.

Maybe Clymer had cached a bottle there. It was worth the try. But only after dark.

Boots grated behind the hiding place. Greer lay down quietly. They were looking for him. It was just like the days when he was a child and he would hear the thud of his father's feet coming up the stairs to make sure Myron wasn't reading in bed. Then Myron would shrink under the covers and draw his legs up towards his belly. He would wrap his arms about himself and lie perfectly still until his father was gone. Slowly he drew up his legs and then wrapped his thin arms about himself. He closed his eyes. Maybe blessed sleep would come this way.

The sun had died in the western skies in a phantasmagoria of pink, rose and gold. The canyon was deep in thickening shadows. Heat still filled the canyon, waiting to be dispersed by the night winds. The five stray horses drifted from in front of the cliff dwellings in search of the *tinaja* further down the canyon. There was plenty of water for them there.

211

Bats flitted through the darkness, emerging from their daylight hiding places. Jack rabbits pattered through the brush and bounded towards the water-hole. Small grey foxes moved about in their ceaseless search for rodents. Kit foxes hunted for mice and lizards along the rock ledges. It was the nocturnal merry-go-round: small animals killed and ate smaller animals only to fall victim to larger predators. The night was the time for the hunter.

Hugh Kinzie wiped the sweat from his face. Chandler Willis shifted his chew and spat. "I ain't seen the little sonofabitch since he relieved me on tower guard so's I could help bury Harry Roswell."

"You don't suppose he's left the dwellings?"

Willis grinned crookedly. "Him? He's got a bottle stashed somewheres. Little bastard wouldn't give me a drink. He'll stay around until he drinks up all the liquor. But even all that rotgut wouldn't make Myron Greer go out into that damned canyon."

Matt Hastings appeared from the darkness and looked at them. "You find him?" he asked.

"No," said Hugh.

Hastings smashed a fist into his other palm. "I'll kick his skinny ass up between his shoulder-blades!" he said.

They began probing into the many empty rooms. Hugh used sotol stalks he had found lying in a pile in one of the rooms, to light his way. He peered into one room after another. Some of them were filled with collapsed roofs, while others were empty as last night's whisky bottle. He could hear the others looking for the frightened little man.

Hugh passed down the triangular passageway. A man came out of the darkness. "What are you doing here?" asked Clymer.

"What the hell do you think I'm doing? Looking for four-leaf clovers?"

Clymer raised his big head. "Some day," he said thickly, "I'll . . ."

"Get out of my way," Hugh said.

"You find Greer?"

213

"If I had I wouldn't be looking for him."

"I'll break his God-damned neck when I get my hands on him."

Hugh shook his head as he walked further up the passageway. Everyone was worried about the missing little man, and yet each of them was threatening death to him if they found him. Hugh almost wished the little man had gone down into the canyon and had died quickly.

Abel Clymer placed a hand on a crumbling wall and swung up on to a pile of roof debris. His big booted feet sank a little into the loose debris. "Greer!" he roared through cupped hands. "Come out! Damn you, I'll flay you alive!"

Five feet below Abel Clymer, Myron Greer raised his head as he heard the muffled voice. Fear settled on Greer like a musty shroud.

Clymer stamped his big feet. "I'll kill him!" he said.

The debris suddenly settled beneath Clymer. Ancient cedar roof beams snapped within the settling debris. One of them sheared off diagonally and slid downward. Its tip penetrated under Greer's left shoulder-blade. The relentless weight of the sinking dried mud and rock drove the sharp tip into Myron Greer's heart.

Maurice Nettleton listened impatiently as Matt Hastings told him of Greer's mysterious disappearance. "Damn it," he snapped. "The man couldn't have left the ruins. He hasn't the guts of a mouse."

"All the same, sir, he can't be found."

Nettleton waved a hand. "Mark him in the book," he said. "Sergeant, someone must make an attempt to break through and bring in help."

Hastings nodded.

Nettleton looked at Hastings' face. "The man who volunteers and succeeds will receive a fitting reward, not to mention the gratitude of my wife and myself."

"I understand, sir."

They eyed each other in the darkness. Nettleton placed a hand on Hastings' shoulder. "I need not tell you that we're in a highly perilous position here, Hastings."

Hastings nodded again. He stepped back and saluted. Then he smartly about-faced and walked away. "The sonofabitch," he said under his breath.

Hastings bent his head to enter the low doorway of the room where Hugh Kinzie and Chandler Willis were waiting for him. Hastings pulled off his shirt and swabbed his armpits with it. "Who's on guard?"

"Morton," said Willis.

"Him? You out of your mind?"

Hugh waved a hand. "He can see and hear even if he is half cracked. What did Nettleton say?"

"Mark him in the book."

Willis scraped at his dirty fingernails with his knife, eyeing Hastings now and then as the first soldier wrote down the entry in his book by the light of a candle stub.

Hastings touched his cracked lips with his tongue. "Greer, M. M., Pvt.—from duty to absent without leave."

Willis leaned forward. "What's the second 'M' stand for, Sarge?"

"Matthias."

Hastings closed the book and looked up at Hugh. "The Old Man wants someone to make a break for help."

"We talked about that before."

Hastings leaned back against the wall, wincing as the hot surface touched his naked back. "I need not tell you that we're in a highly perilous position here, Kinzie."

Hugh looked queerly at the first sergeant.

Hastings grinned. "Those were his last words to me," he said.

"What were your last words to him?" asked Willis.

"The sonofabitch. Only he didn't hear me."

"I wish he had."

Hugh reached behind him and took a bottle out of the pannier. He pried out the wire-wrapped cork. "We'll have a drink on the Old Man," he said.

They drank silently. The bottle went

around three times. Suddenly Willis laughed. The other two looked at him. "Tell us the joke, Willis," said Hastings. "I'd like to laugh too."

Willis grinned. "Captain Nettleton," he said. "First Lieutenant Clymer. Second Lieutenant Phillips. First Sergeant Hastings. Private Willis! You get it?"

The other two looked at each other. Then they began to laugh. "By Jesus," said Hastings. "Just like a damned Mex *revolutionario* army. All officers and noncoms . . . no privates."

Hugh passed the bottle around again. Then he corked it and placed it in a niche. A moment after he did so Darrell Phillips thrust his handsome face into the doorway. "What's going on here?" he asked.

Three innocent faces eyed Darrell Phillips. "Why, sir," said Hastings, "nothing. Nothing at all. We were just having a bit of a joke, as you might say."

Phillips stared at them. "Joking? Here?" He shook his head and vanished into the darkness.

"Maybe we shoulda offered him a drink of the captain's booze," said Hastings.

"To hell with him," said Willis. "He's got something else on his mind."

"Such as?"

"Katy Corse."

Hugh looked quickly at the trooper. "What do you mean?"

Willis grinned. "I seen her switching that little rump of hers at him. She's too good for us. She's working on him. Probably waiting for him somewheres out there in the darkness for a little ride on the two-headed beast."

Hugh moved like a cat. His left hand gripped Willis's shirt front. He dragged the trooper up to his feet. His right hand slashed back and forth from one side to the other until Willis sagged in the grip of Hugh's big hand. Hugh dropped the semi-conscious trooper to the floor and looked down at the bloody ruin he had created. Then he flicked the blood from his hand.

"Hell," said Hastings. He looked down

at Willis and then at Hugh. "You had no call to do that."

The blood mist cleared from Hugh's mind. He snatched up his carbine and walked outside. The liquor was boiling in his mind. He had been a damned fool to drink on an empty stomach. He strode to the tower and climbed up beside Isaiah Morton.

Morton looked at him. "Are we doomed, Mr. Kinzie?" he asked quietly.

"You may be. I'm not."

The first faint light of the moon showed in the sky. Morton looked out at the canyon. "The hand of the Lord was upon me, and carried me out in the spirit of the Lord, and set me down in the midst of the valley which was full of bones.

"And caused me to pass by them round about: and, behold, there were very many in the open valley; and, lo, they were very dry.

"And he said unto me, Son of man, can these bones live? And I answered, O Lord God, thou knowest.

"Again he said unto me, Prophesy

upon these bones and say unto them, O ye dry bones, hear the word of the Lord.

"Thus saith the Lord God unto these bones; Behold, I will cause breath to enter into you, and ye shall live."

Hugh looked down towards the terrace. Katy Corse was with Darrell Phillips. Isaiah Morton raised an admonishing finger. "She doted upon the Assyrians her neighbours, captains and rulers clothed most gorgeously, horsemen riding upon horses, all of them desirable young men.

"Then I saw that she was defiled, that they both took one way."

Hugh turned. "Get to hell out of here," he said thinly. "Gather the canteens and fill them from that water basin."

Morton stepped back.

Hugh drew the fanatical man close to him. "And keep your prophesying to yourself." He shoved the man towards the ladder.

Morton rearranged the front of his coat. He opened his mouth to speak.

"Git!" said Hugh.

Morton climbed clumsily down the chicken ladder.

Hugh looked at Katy and Phillips. The officer was close to her, speaking swiftly and quietly. Hugh gripped the edge of the crumbling window and felt his strength pour out of him as he watched them.

The moon began to silver the sands and etch the shadows of the brush upon them. But there was a different light this night upon the high ground north of the silent canyon—a reddish glow pulsated irregularly against the night. Then the wind began to creep up the canyon, sweeping an odour across the mesas. Not the odour of mesquite and juniper, but the rich odour of roasting meat.

The tempting odour was borne on the wind. It seemed to search with invisible tendrils until it permeated the air throughout the cliff dwellings. Nine people raised their heads and inhaled the titillating scent.

Chandler Willis wiped the blood from his battered face. Matt Hastings had left.

Willis felt for the cached bottle. He drained it and raised his arm to hurl the bottle angrily at the wall. Then he lowered it. A thought that had been in his mind for some time began to take on more important proportions. He stood up and snuffed out the candle. He picked up his carbine and walked out on the terrace. All of them were standing there looking across the canyon to where the glow of the fires illuminated the night sky. The odour of the roasting meat clung tempting and inviting over the ruins.

Willis padded to the back of the tower and looked up at it. He had noticed that Hugh Kinzie was missing. Willis slipped into the lower room and stood there in the darkness listening. He worked his way up to the second floor and waited again. He could hear the gritting of boots on the top floor and the dripping of water in the natural catch basin on the cave wall.

Willis eased up the chicken ladder until he could thrust his head into the floor opening. He could see the broad shoulders of Hugh Kinzie outlined against the window. Willis wet his cracked lips. He rose a little higher.

Hugh Kinzie spoke over his shoulder. "Come on up," he said. "I'm sorry I lost my temper."

Willis climbed up into the room. He leaned his carbine against the wall. Cold sweat soaked through his stinking shirt. The scout must have eyes in the back of his head and ears like a dog.

Willis walked up beside the scout. "I didn't have no call to insult the lady," he said apologetically.

"Forget it."

"Seems like a man talks sometimes without thinking."

"We all do."

"Yeah. Smell the meat?"

"How can you miss it?"

They stood there like two small boys looking into a candy shop window.

Willis looked at Hugh. "You speak Apache?"

"A little."

"You ever been friendly with 'em?"

Hugh looked quickly at Willis. "I've known a few. Why?"

"Nothing. Just wonderin'." Willis cleared his throat. "They all speak the same tongue?"

"There are some dialectal differences, but one of them can usually make his thoughts known to one of another tribal division."

"Supposin' you met one and wanted to be friendly. What would you say?"

Hugh shrugged. "*Nejeunee*. Means good friend, or you could say *scicho*, which means friend. Or *schichobe*, which means, old friend, you behold me!"

"Anything else?" persisted Willis.

"*Sikisn*. Brother."

"Well. Well. You do know something about it. *Gracias, amigo*."

Hugh leaned against the wall and eyed the trooper. "I might add that anyone but an Apache is an enemy. They take no chances."

Willis looked surprised. "I was just curious."

They could hear Morton down in the

225

passageway. The canteens clattered together hollowly. Willis slapped Hugh on the shoulder. "No hard feelin's?"

"None."

"*Gracias*." Willis went down through the hole in the floor.

Hugh scratched his lean jaw. Willis was beginning to act odd, like some of the others.

Isaiah Morton began to fill the first canteen. "And the people thirsted there for water; and the people murmured against Moses, and said, Wherefore is this that thou hast brought us up out of Egypt, to kill us and our children and our cattle with thirst?

"And Moses cried unto the Lord, saying, What shall I do unto this people? they be almost ready to stone me.

"And the Lord said unto Moses, Go on before the people, and take with thee of the elders of Israel; and thy rod, wherewith thou smotest the river, take in thine hand, and go.

"Behold, I will stand before thee there upon the rock in Horeb; and thou shalt smite the rock, and there shall come water out of it, that the people may drink. And Moses did so in the sight of the elders of Israel.

"And he called the name of the place, Massah, and Meribah, because of the chiding of the children of Israel, and because they tempted the Lord, saying, Is the Lord among us, or not?"

15

CHANDLER WILLIS stood for a long time in the shadows. His mind was digesting a daring plan. There was no doubt in him that he must get away from the trap they had all fallen into. There was no organization left; each must look out for himself from now on and to hell with the hindmost. Besides, he was the only flunky left of the group which had entered the canyon of waiting death.

Those Apaches were smart. They hadn't lost a warrior in the whole process. All they had to do was sit where they were and wait for the White-eyes to die of starvation, then move in and gather up the spoils. They already had the horses and mules. It was a cinch.

Willis touched his bruised face. He hadn't expected the attack from Hugh Kinzie but he should have known better.

Willis had never really expected Kinzie to throw in with him, and now he was sure about it.

Hunger pains gnawed at his belly. It was time to pull foot. He'd try to work his way out of the canyon. If he was seen he'd talk to the Mimbrenos in the words taught him by Hugh Kinzie. He'd offer them liquor he'd steal from Nettleton's cache. He'd make it all right.

Willis slipped into the little room where Harry Roswell had died because he had obeyed his orders. Willis slid two bottles inside his filthy shirt. He hooked his canteens to his belt and walked outside. Katy Corse and Darrell Phillips were still talking. Hell of a place for dallying. There was no one else in sight. The wind carried the inviting odour of roast meat to him.

Willis walked to the west end of the terrace. Hugh Kinzie was talking with Isaiah Morton. Willis eased over the crumbling wall and stood in a shadow, listening. Hugh Kinzie moved around in the tower room. Willis dropped to his belly, cradling his carbine in the crooks of his elbows, then worked his way under cover down the slope until he reached a place where a jungle of rocks and brush allowed him to stand up without being seen. He looked back at the dwellings, then thumbed his nose at them. Then he was gone through the thick brush, padding his way silently towards the huge rock shoulder which hid so many secrets from the people in the cliff dwellings.

Katy Corse stood at the edge of the terrace feeling the warm wind move her sweat-damp hair. It was the heat more than the hunger which bothered Katy; Darrell Phillips bothered her more than both of them together.

Darrell Phillips stood with bowed head, hands gripping the crumbling top of the wall. There was a sickness in him at being trapped in this alien place, with blood-thirsty primitives waiting out there in the shadows to kill, torture and rape.

The two of them had been standing there for three-quarters of an hour at least, and Darrell Phillips had been doing most of the talking.

Katy placed a hand on his shoulder. "You're really frightened, aren't you, Darrell?"

He raised his head. "In a way. Aren't you?"

She shrugged. "Yes. But it seems deeper in you."

He came closer to her. "You do understand me, then! You want to understand me."

She smiled a little. "You mean no one understands you?"

He flushed. "Not like that. It just seems that you do more than the others."

She nodded and looked out across the canyon. It was always so. Officers came and went, and more than half of them she had met had told her, or intimated the same thing. But once they had left for duty in other parts, she had been completely forgotten. It had happened a number of times before. If she survived from this experience, it would happen again.

Phillips turned his back on the brooding moonlit canyon. "I keep trying to people the canyon," he said quietly.

"Yes. It seems as though the shadows and the moving brush are like figures from a Walpurgis Night."

He shivered a little. "With the Beltane fires glowing on the heights."

"You mustn't let your imagination run riot."

"How can I prevent it?"

She tilted her head to one side. "You should never have become a soldier."

He jerked his head and looked at her. "I've always wanted to be a soldier, Katy."

"Why? To prove to everyone that you're not afraid?"

It was as though she had driven a needle bayonet into him. He gripped her by the arms. "No! Katy, it's one thing to face white men in civilized warfare and quite another to fight against these human tigers. I've heard stories of what they do to captives. It makes me sick inside. So sick that I can't think clearly. Believe me when I say that I'm not a coward. You must believe me!"

She looked up into his face. "Yes," she said softly.

"I can lead a charge against breast-works and never falter. I can stand artillery fire and the volley of musketry. I'm not afraid of hand-to-hand combat with sword and pistol. But this is breaking me down. The eternal waiting. The silence. The deaths of Pearce, Stevens and Roswell, and the disappearance of Greer. Almost as though death is standing in the shadows, reaching out now and then with a bony finger to tap each one of us on the shoulder. It might be you next. It might be me."

She touched his flushed face. "Control yourself."

He placed his hand over hers and pressed it close to his cheek. "Katy," he said tensely, "it isn't the thought of dying that frightens me. It's the *way* of dying."

His body began to shake. Tears filled his eyes. She took him by the hand and led him to one of the rooms. She sat down on the floor and drew him down to her. He placed his head on her lap. His sobs came at regular intervals.

Hugh Kinzie watched Katy and Darrell Phillips enter the dwelling. It seemed as though a vial of acid had been broken inside of him. For a moment he thought of going down there and killing Darrell Phillips, but then he got control of himself.

It was quiet; it was too damned quiet.

Hugh Kinzie raised his head. He couldn't see or hear anything, but he could sense something about to happen.

Chandler Willis padded across the canyon seeking the shelter of the great shoulder of rock which projected into the canyon. There was no sign of life other than the occasional scuttering of a small nocturnal animal.

Cold sweat worked down his sides and greased his carbine stock beneath the grip of his hands. His head turned constantly from side to side as he advanced. Something seemed to warn him to go back, but he could not force himself to do so once he had made his decision to desert. He wasn't really deserting, he assured himself. He was just looking out for Number One.

Marion Nettleton stirred restlessly in her sleep. Maurice Nettleton raised himself on an elbow and looked down at her. She was getting thin. There were dark circles beneath her lovely eyes. The sands of time were running out on the trapped party. Maurice Nettleton placed his hand on his Colt. There would be one shot for her, and he hoped to God he would have time to kill her before they got hold of her. Then he hoped he would have time to kill himself so that he wouldn't have time to think of the horrible thing he had been forced to do.

Abel Clymer was eating. He crouched in the triangular passageway, feeling the sweat run down his face as he spooned greasy tough meat into his mouth from a can of embalmed beef. He had cached three cans of the repulsive stuff so that he would be able to keep strength in his body for the time when he would make his break with Marion Nettleton. He glanced at the debris pile to his left. Under it was something else he had to take along.

Isaiah Morton placed the canteens in one of the rooms. He felt no hunger. He was used to fasting and self-torture in his effort to eliminate the thoughts of bodily comfort from his mind, leaving it free for the work of the Lord. He squatted in the dimness and began to pray.

Matt Hastings was cleaning his weapons. He jerked the pull-through out of his carbine barrel and held the weapon up to the light of the moon to check the barrel.

Two Colts, loaded and capped, lay on his blanket, freshly cleaned and oiled. He loaded his carbine and capped it. Then he took out his sheath knife and began to sharpen it. The steady *wheet-wheet-wheet* of steel against stone kept time to his thoughts. No damned greasy Mimbreno was going to get Matt Hastings without a hell of a fracas. He'd take enough of them along with him to act as his pallbearers to hell.

Chandler Willis was almost around the rock shoulder, holding his breath, hoping to God that the canyon wasn't a box.

The warrior materialized from the brush almost as though raised from a prone position by the strings of a master puppeteer. He was fifty feet from Chandler Willis. He did not move, but watched the white man with great liquid eyes.

Willis stopped with one foot planted forward. His carbine was in the crook of his left arm. He slowly extended his right hand, palm towards the silent buck. "*Nejeunee,*" he said clearly.

The warrior stood there as though carved from the very rocks behind him.

Chandler Willis swallowed dryly. "*Schicho!*" he said.

The wind moaned about the rock shoulder. The warrior stood like a statue.

Willis raised his head. "*Schichobe!*" he mouthed.

The musket roared inches from the back of the deserter's head, smashing in the back of his skull. The blood sprayed out and stained the clean sands. Chandler Willis was dead before he knew what had hit him.

The crashing discharge of the big musket slammed back and forth between the canyon walls and then slowly died away down the canyon. The warrior lowered his smoking weapon and hooked a toe under the dead man's body. He rolled him over. Willis's arms flung outward. The killer spat and looked at his mate. "*Nejeunee! Schicho! Schichobe!*" he said.

The two Mimbrenos laughed.

The killer lifted his buckskin kilt and slapped his naked haunch. He spat on the body. "*Yah-tats-ar!*" he said.

Hugh Kinzie ran to the terrace wall and looked in the direction from which the gunshot had come. Matt Hastings stopped beside him. "What is it?" he asked.

"*Quién sabe?*"

Nettleton came to them. "Who was it?"

Hugh looked along the terrace. Marion Nettleton was leaning against a dwelling wall. Isaiah Morton was beside her. Katy Corse stood beside Darrell Phillips. He had his arm around her waist. Abel Clymer walked out of a passageway and stopped behind Hugh. Hugh caught the odour of food on the big officer's breath.

"Where's Willis?" asked Hastings suddenly.

They all looked at each other, then looked down the quiet canyon. "Mark it in the book, Matt," said Hugh.

"You're sure?"

Hugh nodded. "He wanted to know how to say a friendly greeting to them," he said.

"He got his answer the hard way," said Hastings, wetting his cracked lips. "I'll mark it down." He looked at Hugh. "He didn't have any middle initial," he said. He walked to his quarters.

Maurice Nettleton walked slowly back to his wife. His shoulders were rounded. He silently took her by the arm and led her into their quarters.

Darrell Phillips turned suddenly and walked to the far end of the terrace.

Katy Corse looked at Phillips, then walked towards Hugh.

Katy stopped beside Hugh. "Was it Willis?"

"I haven't any doubt about it," he said coldly.

She placed a hand on his arm. "What's wrong, Hugh?"

"Go back to him," he said, jerking a thumb at Phillips.

"What do you mean?"

There was a sneer on his face as he looked down at her. "You didn't have much time to get anything done with him in that room," he said.

Her right hand lashed his face. She turned on a heel and ran to her quarters.

Far down the canyon a coyote gave voice and was answered by one of his mates.

16

THE moon was on the wane. The cliff dwellings seemed as deserted as they had been before the arrival of the party. Hugh padded back into the triangular passageway. He walked softly along it until he found a place where something lay on the ground. He knelt and looked at it. It was a piece of ragged tin. He fingered it, rubbing grease from it. He sniffed at his fingers. Embalmed beef. Hugh stood up and looked about. Clymer had been eating recently. No one else had a scrap of food.

Hugh looked at a debris pile. It looked as though it had been disturbed. He began to remove rocks. Something grated on the ground behind him. He whirled in time to have a big fist driven hard against his jaw. He went down hard and hit his head against a rock. He tried to get up but Clymer drove a boot against his side.

Hugh grunted in pain. He rolled away from the big man and got to his feet in time to meet a smashing attack. Clymer drove in piston-like blows, battering alternately at Hugh's face and belly, until Hugh was driven back into a corner where the rock wall of the cave met the end of the row of dwellings. Hugh's head bounced from the wall. He covered up and worked his way around the officer.

Clymer danced about on his big feet. "You sonofabitch," he said thickly. "You nosy bastard!"

Clymer drove in hard again. Hugh parried the blows with elbows and forearms. The very weight and speed of Clymer's attack began to work against him. Hugh drove in a hard left jab, snapping Clymer's head back. He followed through with a smash low to the belly. Clymer grunted. He staggered back with his arms outflung, allowing Hugh time to close in hard and fast, driving blows to the belly.

Clymer hit the wall. He got in one good punch but paid a high price for it. Hugh swung from the waist, uppercutting the big man. Teeth and lips smashed together. Hugh planted a right over Clymer's heart. The big man bent forward in time to catch a neat uppercut. He sagged and slid down to the floor.

Hugh stepped back. "You loco bastard," he said thickly.

Clymer ran a hand across his battered mouth and flicked the blood against the rock wall. He shook his head and got up on his feet. Then he hunched forward, dropping his right hand to his pistol. Hugh clamped his left hand on Clymer's right wrist. He sank his right fist deep into Clymer's belly. The officer's sour breath exploded into Hugh's face. He grunted in pain. Hugh dropped his hand to his own Colt and freed it from its holster. He rammed the muzzle into Clymer's belly and looked into the wide, frightened eyes. "You sonofabitch," he said quietly, "I'd like to cut you down to size."

Hastings and Nettleton came up behind

Hugh. "What is this, sir?" snapped Nettleton.

Hugh stepped to one side but kept his revolver in his hand. The big man had shaken him badly, and Hugh began to feel weak from the lack of food.

Clymer looked at Nettleton. "This man attacked me in here for no reason that I know of, sir. The man is demented."

Nettleton looked steadily at Hugh. "What have you to say for yourself, sir?"

Hugh shrugged. "I was looking around back here. Clymer jumped me for no reason at all."

"Is this true, Mr. Clymer?" asked Nettleton.

"No."

"He knows why I was looking around back here," said Hugh.

"Well?" demanded Nettleton of Clymer.

Clymer wet his thick lips. He looked away from his commanding officer. "I had a little food cached back here," he said.

Nettleton raised his head. "Food? All

supplies were to be turned in to Sergeant Hastings. You deliberately disobeyed my orders, sir!"

Clymer swelled up his chest. "I'm a big man, sir. The biggest of all of you. I wanted to keep strength in my body for our escape, knowing it would depend on me to get Mrs. Nettleton to safety."

Nettleton raised a shaking hand. "You will consider yourself under arrest, Mr. Clymer."

Clymer stared at him. Then he laughed. "Under arrest? Where will you put me, sir?" He laughed again and swung out a thick arm to indicate the canyon. "We're all prisoners, you pompous idiot! With dozens of jailors thirsting for our blood! Damn you, Nettleton! You got us into this. Now let a better man get you out of this unholy mess!" Clymer stalked off.

Hugh rubbed his battered jaw. Suspicion began to form in his mind. Clymer wasn't gutty enough to kill a man for a can of embalmed beef. There was something else he was hiding.

Nettleton looked as though he had been kicked in the belly. He looked at Hugh and then at Hastings. "We'll say no more about this," he said.

Hugh nodded.

Nettleton hesitated. "Did you find any food? Not for myself, you understand," he said hastily, "but for Mrs. Nettleton."

Hugh shook his head. "Nor any for Miss Corse, either," he said.

Nettleton jerked his head as though he had been slapped. "Yes. Yes. Of course." He placed a hand on Hugh's arm. "Tell me, Kinzie: is there a chance of escape?"

Hugh looked down at him. "I don't know."

"Will you try to get a message through?"

"If I can get out of this canyon, sir, it would be days before I could bring back help. If I did bring back help, what would we find when we got here?"

Nettleton nodded. "Yes," he said quietly. "Of course." He turned away and walked out towards the terrace.

Hastings eyed Hugh. "Now how about the truth, Hugh?"

"Damned if I know. I knew Clymer had been eating. I came in here and found a piece of tin from a beef can. I was poking around to find his cache when he got me from behind."

"I wish you'd killed the big stud."

Hugh felt his jaw. "He damned near killed me."

Hastings looked down the passageway and spoke in a low voice. "Watch your back, Hugh."

Hugh nodded. "What are we doing to do now, Matt?"

Hastings spat. "I'm not going to sit here to be caught like a rat."

"So?"

Hastings raised his head. "No gut-eating Apache is going to crack my skull to keep my spirit from haunting him."

Hugh looked closely at the veteran. "I'll need you when the time comes to make the break. You're the only one I can trust now, Matt."

Hastings stepped back. "Yeah." He walked away.

Hugh stared at the first soldier. A subtle change had come over Hastings.

Hugh walked towards the tower. He stopped in the semi-circular area at the west end of the passageway. His boots crunched ancient maize cobs. He looked up at the rock fault which had been carefully sealed with rocks and mortar. Then he looked up at the cave ceiling. It must be many yards thick between the ceiling and the mesa top. He looked at the sealed fault again. He passed a hand over the smooth surface of the mortared rocks. They had taken great pains to seal it off. What was behind it?

Hugh climbed up into the tower and walked across the beam they had placed to reach the water pan. He placed a hand in the thin sheet of water and pressed its coolness against his aching face. He squatted there in the dimness, wishing for a smoke. His head throbbed. It was hard to think. He eyed the glistening trickle of water. It seemed to come from the very pores of the rock itself. He crawled over to it and pressed a hand against it, trying to fathom from whence it came. He looked up at the rock roof again. How many yards to the mesa floor?

Hugh closed his eyes. A faintness seemed to come over him. He tried to shake it off. The fight had taken a hell of a lot of strength out of him.

He walked across the narrow bridge they had made to reach the water. He stepped down from the window ledge and full into a soft body. Marion Nettleton slid her arms about his neck. "Are you all right, Hugh? I couldn't rest when Maurice told me what had happened."

He looked down at her. The faint odour of rich perfume came from her.

"Hugh, is there any chance for us at all?" she whispered.

"All I have to have happen now is to have the captain walk in on us."

She shook her head. "He's lying down. He broods a lot. Hugh, he can't get me out of here."

"And you think *I* can?"

She moved closer and the faintly sour odour of her sweat came to him mingled with the rich perfume. Hugh almost grinned. Marion Nettleton wasn't going to stink like the rest of the common folk. But the combination of odours was typical of her. There was a stink behind her looks and polish. He took her arms from around his neck.

"When the time comes, Marion, we'll all know who is going to be saved. Like Resurrection Day."

She replaced her arms about his neck and pressed her lower body hard against his. "Don't send me away," she said softly.

Hugh was tempted. The sands of time were trickling away fast and it had been a long time since he had had a woman, and the last one he had had wasn't in a class with Marion Nettleton, except that she had had some sense of honour despite her moral code. "You'd better get back to your husband," he said.

For a moment she hesitated. Hugh almost took her then and there, but she turned away and left the room. He shrugged and followed her. Katy Corse came out of the shadows and looked up at him. "You didn't have much time to get anything done with her in that tower," she said.

Hugh scratched his jaw. Then he smiled. He broke into a wide grin and then laughed aloud. He swept her to him and kissed her hard. Then he pushed her away. "Can *he* kiss you like that, Katy? Tell the truth?"

She bit her lip. "Damn you, Hugh Kinzie," she said. She walked to her quarters.

Darrell Phillips stepped out in front of Hugh as he followed Katy. "Where are you going?" he asked quietly.

"None of your damned business, Phillips."

"I can't fight you as Clymer did, but I can ask you out as a gentleman!"

Hugh grinned again. "Hell, but everybody is touchy tonight. She's all yours, Phillips."

Phillips watched Hugh walk to the far

end of the terrace. Abel Clymer came out of his room and stopped beside Phillips. "Some day I'll break his damned back," he said.

Phillips glanced at the big man. "If he doesn't break yours first, Clymer. I almost wish to God he had."

Clymer turned quickly. "I'll smash your pretty face," he snarled.

Phillips stepped back. "I'll put a bullet into your belly first, Clymer."

Clymer glanced down at Phillips's gun. Then he looked into the taut, cold face. "There'll be a showdown before long," he said. "Then all these little problems will be settled. Sweet hell, Phillips, I'd like to see those Apache squaws working over you with knife and fire."

Phillips went pale. He bit his lip and turned away. A sour flood seemed to rise in his throat. Behind him Abel Clymer laughed aloud.

17

DARRELL PHILLIPS had the guard just before dawn. A cold wind swept through the canyon just as the first traces of the false dawn tinged the eastern skies. He shivered a little and drew his blanket about his shoulders. There was a dull gnawing ache in the pit of his stomach, and his head throbbed a little. He had amused himself during his watch by thinking of the fine restaurants he had dined in back east. A poor way for a half-starved man to spend his time.

He felt better with the coming of light, for the darkness was peopled with phantoms who seemed to leer and gibber at him from behind every rock and clump of brush.

He hunched his shoulders beneath the blanket and thought of Katy Corse. It was she who had brought him the blanket as he had gone on watch. She was trying to understand him in the goodness of her heart. It was his damned imagination that caused him so much trouble. It had always been so. The actuality had always been less fearful than the expectancy. She had placed a probing finger on his secret. She knew why he had become a soldier. To prove to the world that he had courage. He knew he wasn't really a coward. Not as much as some men, in any case. Somehow he had thought that wearing blue and brass would prove to everyone that he was as brave as any man. He had seen little action at Fort Ayres, but what he had seen after several slashing Apache raids on stage stations and lonely ranches had been branded on his mind with letters of fire. There seemed to be a thick green mucous of fear clogging his soul.

The light was better now. He looked down the slope. There was a strange growth there. Something alien. He stared at it, and then opened his mouth. A shriek that did not seem to emanate from his mouth awoke the canyon echoes. It was almost as though someone else had done it.

Hugh Kinzie burst from his room holding his Sharps carbine at hip level. He stared at Phillips's ghastly white face. The officer dropped his carbine, pointed down the slope, then turned away to retch violently.

Hugh looked down the slope. A white man lay there, stripped to the buff. His head was curiously misshapen. It was Chandler Willis—or what had been Chandler Willis.

Hugh gripped Phillips by the shoulder. "Make sure the women don't see this." He shoved Phillips towards the dwellings. The officer walked as though in a dream, dropping the blanket from his shoulders.

Matt Hastings came up at a trot and looked down at Willis. "I knew it," he said.

Hugh nodded. "At least he wasn't tortured," he said.

Hastings spat dryly. "For Pete's sake,

Hugh, if they get at me and wound me, make damned sure you save a slug for me. You'll remember that?"

"Yes."

"I'll do the same for you."

"*Gracias*," said Hugh dryly.

"I'll go down and noose a picket line on his body. We can draw him up here and bury him."

Maurice Nettleton looked down at the body. "When did they put him there?"

"*Quién sabe?*" said Hugh. "The point is that they dragged that body clear across the canyon and placed him not thirty feet from the man standing on guard."

Nettleton touched his throat. There was a sickness apparent on his face. "If I had only tried with all speed for the Rio Grande," he said.

"You didn't."

"We might have been safely at Santa Fe now."

Hugh spat over the wall. "It's a little late to think about it now."

Hastings passed them carrying a coiled

picket line in his hand. He vaulted the wall and slid down the slope. He worked quickly, glancing now and then over his shoulder. Hugh knelt behind the wall with his cocked carbine in his hands, watching the opposite canyon wall.

Hastings finished. He came up the slope, uncoiling the line. They pulled the battered corpse up to the wall and lifted it over. Hugh looked away from the smashed head.

They buried Chandler Willis in a hole behind one of the buildings. Abel Clymer leaned against the wall watching them as they finished the burial. Hastings marked it in the book. "I had a feeling he'd make a break," said Matt Hastings.

Hugh nodded. "Five down; eight to go, as *he* would have said."

"At least he's out of this mess."

Hugh scratched the bristles on his face. "The chips are all down now, Matt."

Hastings leaned back against a wall. There were dark circles under his eyes, and his uniform was beginning to hang loosly on his thick body. "If we didn't have the women," he said quietly, "we could all make a break for it. We're all handy with sidearms. Except Morton. I'd rather die fighting than like a rat in a trap."

"We can't leave the women, Matt."

They looked at each other.

"It isn't time yet," said Hugh. "Besides . . . who would do it? Roswell might have; he always obeyed orders. I'll not do it until the last possible moment."

Hastings touched his cracked lips. "We can draw straws."

"I said I wouldn't do it now!"

"We can make it easy on them. A bullet in the back of the head when they don't expect it."

"No!"

"Look, Hugh! We won't all get out of this mess. Six men might make it after dark. Sure, some of us will get it. But I'm enough of a gambler to take my chance. One man might break free. I'll take those odds against sitting there waiting for the end. Another day of this and we'll all be too weak to make a mile on foot."

Hugh watched Clymer walking towards the watch-tower. "Clymer could."

Hastings figured the butt of his Colt. "I once thought I'd plug him in the back in the first action we got into."

"Our loss would be Heaven's gain, as Isaiah would say. Let's go and talk with the others."

They gathered in front of the watch-tower as the sun began to flood the canyon. Nettleton's hands shook as he buttoned up his blouse despite the heat. Clymer squatted with his back against the tower. There was a set look on his broad face. Phillips seemed pale beneath his tanned face. Now and again he wet his lips and looked across the empty canyon. Hastings stood up with his big hands folded atop his carbine muzzle. Isaiah Morton was there in body only.

Nettleton looked about. "We must do something," he said nervously. "My wife is not well. There is no food left."

"No horses either," said Clymer.

"Yes. Yes."

"If you had listened to me, we would have made a break out of here some days ago," said Clymer.

"Let us look forward, Mr. Clymer."

Clymer laughed. "To what?"

"I wanted to make a sortie then," said Darrell Phillips.

"Yeah," said Clymer. "You were going with the captain here as *aide*. Who was detailed to lead the attack? Me! Well, I'm not leading any attack now, sonny."

"We haven't enough strength in numbers for that now," said Nettleton.

They looked at each other. None of them had an idea. The realization that death was a surety instead of an even chance weighed on them.

Isaiah Morton opened his eyes. "Perhaps we could reason with our red brethren. Surely there is some pity in them. Are they not the Lord's children as well as we?"

"You talk with them," said Clymer.

"Yes! I am willing."

"He don't talk their lingo," said Hastings.

"Kinzie does," said Clymer slyly.

They all looked at Hugh. He shook his head. "They're out for our blood."

Phillips walked to the edge of the terrace. "Perhaps, after dark, before the moon rises, we could scale this side of the canyon and pull the ladies up by means of the picket ropes."

Nettleton rubbed his jaw. "Perhaps. What do the rest of you think?"

"Sounds all right, sir," said Hastings, "but maybe they're up there too."

"Yes," said Nettleton. He paced back and forth. "But we can try. Yes! We'll do it!"

Hugh shrugged. "It's our last chance," he said. He studied the others.

Clymer stood up. "I'll go," he said.

Hastings nodded. "Count me in, sir."

Isaiah Morton wandered off. He looked out across the canyon. Voices seemed to speak into his ears. Hunger and thirst were forgotten as he walked back and forth, trying to clearly understand the words which he heard. He stopped and stood at the edge of the terrace for a long time staring at the motionless brush which rimmed the edge of the far canyon wall.

18

THEY worked swiftly in the gathering dusk. There was no dissension amongst them now. Picket lines were tied together and coiled. Picket pins were bundled together so that they could be carried easily to where they would be wedged into rock crevices as improvised pitons. Clymer carried the bundle of pins. Phillips carried the coiled picket lines. Hastings was the only one who carried a carbine, as he had added another Colt to his armament. Nettleton was to stay with the women. Hugh was to scale the canyon side. Morton had vanished into the ruins to commune with his Lord and himself.

Hugh had stripped off his shirt and had removed his boots. He expected to cut the very devil out of his feet, but they would be surer than his heavy boots. He led the way to the west end of the terrace and eased over the wall, followed by the others. Hugh padded along the slope and stopped fifty yards from the end of the ruins. He looked up at the canyon wall. One place was as good as another. Phillips and Clymer came softly up to Hugh in the darkness. Hastings faded down the slope and took up a position where he could cover the approaches to the ruins and the scaling party.

Hugh worked his way up a tip-tilted slab of rock. He stopped at the top and strained his eyes upwards, studying the rock formations above him. The wall was solid looking, but there were places where frost and rain had hastened the work of decomposition. Hugh reached back and took the ends of the coiled lines from Phillips. The young officer was breathing harshly. Clymer handed Hugh one of the picket pins. He fastened the bundle to a spare picket line and fastened the free end to Hugh's belt.

Hugh felt the cliff face. It was solid enough. He began to work his way upwards, sweating coldly at the thought of having one of the picket pins clash against the cliff.

He cursed as he placed his hand in a clump of catclaw growing in a thin pocket of soil on a ledge. His hand smarted like fire as he climbed up. He was up fifty feet before he had to wedge a picket pin into a crevice for a foothold. He worked slowly, breathing quickly as he worked the tip of the pin into a solid position. He pulled himself up a little and tested his weight on the pin. It gave a little, and then held. He pulled himself up higher by a hand-hold and rested a foot on the pin. He felt the bundle of picket pins drag a little at the end of the line fastened to his belt.

A faint wind carried down the canyon, bearing the sweetish odour of decomposition with it. Hugh wiped the sweat from his stinging face. It must be Dan Pearce making himself known as the cooling night air contracted his gas-swollen belly.

Hugh worked up on to a narrow transverse ledge and felt for another handhold. The dull buzzing warned him and he jerked back his hand as something struck just where it had been. The rank odour of the rattler tainted his nostrils. He pulled back his head, trying to spot the scaly body. There was a rustling movement and then a dull scraping noise. Sweat began to drip into his eyes.

Some damned fool down below tugged at the line fastened to Hugh's belt. His foot slipped and he was forced to grab for the ledge again. His fingers closed on something scaly, and he felt the hard rattle buttons beneath his fingers. There was no time to think or jump. He gripped hard just above the rattles and jerked the thick heavy body from the ledge. As it reached full length he snapped hard. The rattler hung lifeless in his hand. Pebbles and dirt pattered down far below him. He heard a muffled curse.

Hugh hung there by one hand, feeling his foot slip on the lower ledge. He wanted to drop the heavy rattler but he knew damned well if that cold body struck one of those nerve-taut men below, unadulterated hell would break loose for sure. Juggling the rattler with one hand, he gripped tight with the other and then swung the limp body up on to the ledge where it struck heavily. Then he followed it, dropping flat on top of it, feeling the cold scales beneath his naked chest and belly.

A greenish sickness came over him. He wondered how much worse things could get before he escaped or earned the blessed oblivion of death.

He figured he was up at least sixty feet. Mentally he calculated that the ceiling of the great cave which housed the ruins was at least eighty to one hundred feet above the tallest structure. Then the top of the mesa was at least thirty to forty feet higher than that. He shook his head, then wiped his bleeding palms against the rough material of his trousers. He felt weak and lightheaded, and he rested his head against the warm rock, fighting off vertigo which came and went spasmodically.

He felt for the line which hung from his belt and began to pull up the heavy bundle of picket pins, easing it when the bundle began to swing too much, trying to get a straight vertical pull. The picket line cut into his raw palms and the salt of his sweat made them feel as though he were dipping them into acid.

He felt the bundle bump the edge of the ledge and he pulled it up beside him. A small rock was brushed over the edge. It bounded from a projection and then struck sharply far below. He lay still, listening with all his power.

Isaiah Morton stood by the terrace wall. The darkness was so thick that it could almost be felt. He thrust out a gaunt hand encrusted with dirt and pawed at the darkness as though he could rift it sufficiently to see the far side of the canyon. "My heart is sore pained within me: and the terrors of death are fallen upon me.

"Fearfulness and trembling are come upon me, and horror hath overwhelmed me.

"And I said, Oh that I had wings like

a dove! for then would I fly away, and be at rest.

"Lo, then would I wander far off, and remain in the wilderness. Selah!"

Katy Corse sat with her elbows resting on her knees and her hands cupping her oval face. She looked straight ahead, almost unaware of Marion Nettleton who sat across from her. Now and then Marion's dry sobbing drifted to Katy through the haze which seemed to envelop her. The sobbing grew louder. "Be quiet!" hissed Katy.

"I'm afraid."

"Who isn't?"

"But it affects me worse than it does you, Katy."

"Maybe. I'm thinking of those men out there, risking their lives for us."

"It's their duty."

Katy dropped her hands. "You *would* think so. Don't you ever think of anyone but yourself?"

Marion bit her lip. "You're talking to a lady, Katy Corse."

Katy stared at her, then threw back her head and began to laugh.

Marion closed her hand on a stone; it would be so easy to close her mouth. "If it weren't for you," she said quietly, "the men might have been able to get me out of here. Hugh Kinzie can do it."

"And have himself killed? I'd rather have him leave me and save himself."

"Why don't you get Darrell Phillips to save you? You certainly threw yourself at him! I'd laugh if it weren't so tragic. You . . . a frontier doxie, thinking Darrell Phillips is really interested in you."

Katy stood up. She clenched her hands. For a moment she almost reached down to grip Marion by the hair and drag her to her feet. "I often wondered how deep your breeding went," she said quietly. "I can see now that it's pitifully thin veneer."

"Ladies!" hissed Maurice Nettleton from the doorway. "You must be quiet!"

Marion glanced sideways at her

271

husband and then up at Katy. "We'll take this up some other time," she promised.

Katy laughed. "Any time."

Maurice Nettleton shook his head. He walked to the edge of the terrace. He could hear Isaiah Morton mumbling another of his eternal prayers. "Be quiet!" said Maurice Nettleton out of the darkness. "Those men are trying to save our lives!"

Isaiah held up his thin arms. "Cast thy burden upon the Lord, and He shall sustain thee: He shall never suffer the righteous to be moved!"

Nettleton drew out his pistol and cocked it. "Damn you! You and your prating and praying! You should be on guard here while I should be out there helping them! Now keep your mouth shut at least!" Nettleton turned and hastened to the west end of the terrace to see if there was any sign of progress.

Morton thrust an accusing finger towards Nettleton. "But Thou, O God, shalt bring them down into the pit of destruction: bloody and deceitful men shall not live out half their days: but I will trust in Thee."

Hugh Kinzie stood up on the ledge and felt above him. He was sick with horror that he might touch another diamondback and run out of what little luck he had left. His hands scrabbled in vain. He felt for a picket pin and inserted it into three different crevices until it seemed to hold firm. He looked back over his shoulder. There was a faint greyish-yellow tinge in the eastern sky. The moon was slowly rising. He worked slowly, forcing himself to remain calm as he worked up the cliff.

He was a good forty feet from the top when he suddenly became aware that he could see better. He looked back. The canyon was still in deep shadow. But the eastern sky was lighting.

He clung to a picket pin. He looked up. He was sure he could make it by himself and still not be seen by the prying eyes of the Mimbrenos. The temptation was strong. The odds of getting the rest of them out were hopelessly high. He closed his eyes and rested flat against the cliff face.

It would take him another half-hour to reach the top. By that time he could be seen against the cliff face. But he could go over the top and make tracks during the night until he was free at last from their almost unseen captors.

Hugh Kinzie slowly wiped the sweat from his face with his free hand. It was no use. He couldn't do it. He'd have to go down now and they'd have to wait until the moon was gone to finish building their perilous ladder to freedom.

Hugh felt for the pin under him and eased himself down until he reached the upper ledge. He picked up the body of the snake and tied it behind him. Then he felt for a foothold. The moon was beginning to light the canyon. Already he could distinguish the slope below the terrace. There was something moving there.

The clear voice came up to him and

echoed through the canyon. "Hear my cry, O God; attend unto my prayer.

"From the end of the earth will I cry unto Thee, when my heart is overwhelmed: lead me to the rock that is higher than I.

"For Thou hast been a shelter for me, and a strong tower from the enemy.

"I will abide in Thy tabernacle forever: I will trust in the cover of Thy wings. Selah!"

There was a muffled exclamation below Hugh. Then boots smashed against the earth. Rocks began to roll down the slope.

Hugh looked back. Isaiah Morton was walking down the slope with arms held high above his head.

There was a flare of light from the far side of the canyon. Then a faggot curved gracefully through the darkness, trailing a stream of sparks. It struck in the thick dry brush and scattered bits of burning wood. In a moment the brush caught the flame and began to burn swiftly. The light showed Isaiah Morton walking confidently towards the west end of the great canyon.

Phillips and Clymer were running for the cliff dwellings. Then rifles began to crash from the northern rim of the canyon, kicking up spurts of dust close to the two officers.

Hastings stood up. "Hugh! I'll cover you! Come on! Shake the dust!"

Isaiah Morton walked through the flaming brush, seemingly in a trance. The Mimbrenos did not fire at him. Instead they poured their fire towards the two officers who were scrambling over the wall. Slugs whispered through the smoke and slapped against the dwellings. Nettleton fired wildly, at an impossible range for his six-gun.

Hastings looked up at Hugh with wild eyes. "Damn it! Come on!"

Morton walked on through the crashing hell of the rifles and the crackling of the flames. "The Lord is my shepherd; I shall not want.

"He maketh me to lie down in green

pastures: He leadeth me beside the still waters.

"He restoreth my soul: He leadeth me in the paths of righteousness for His name's sake."

Hugh jumped from the last ledge and slid down the tip-tilted slab of rock. Slugs slapped against the canyon wall. Hastings fired his carbine and swiftly reloaded. Then he stood up and looked back at Hugh. "Run, you bastard! Run!"

Morton stumbled and fell. He got up and walked on.

"Yea, though I walk through the valley of the shadow of death, I will fear no evil: for Thou art with me; Thy rod and Thy staff they comfort me."

Hugh snatched up the coiled line and the remainder of the picket pins. He plunged into the brush. The flames were roaring and dancing, casting weird shadows and spurts of reflected light from the canyon walls. It was as bright as day.

Hastings fired his carbine. Slugs smashed into him. He walked forward with a Colt in either hand, staggering a little as more slugs smashed into him. His body jerked. "You red bastards!" he yelled. "I'm coming! I'm coming!"

Hugh tripped and fell behind a rock ledge. He lay still as rifles crackled in harmony with the blazing brush. Someone yelled from the cliff dwellings. Carbines began to rattle from the terrace wall.

Hastings was reeling across the bright canyon floor, pumping alternate shots from both Colts. Half-way across the canyon he pitched forward on his face and lay still. His body jerked as slugs pounded into it.

Isaiah Morton was almost to the granite shoulder. He turned and looked back. "Surely goodness and mercy shall follow me all the days of my life: and I will dwell in the house of the Lord forever."

Then he was gone into the shadow beneath the rock shoulder.

Hugh raised his head. The flames had died away leaving red ember eyes winking on the canyon floor. It was quiet again. The odour of burnt cloth, brush and flesh mingled with the acrid gunpowder smoke.

He hunched himself along behind the ledge, stopping and listening now and then. The silence had descended again after the savage outburst of musketry.

Hugh worked his way up the slope. There was a scuffling of feet behind the terrace wall. A head appeared. Hugh rolled over behind a bush and waited. A carbine cracked flatly, awakening the echoes again. The report seemed to bounce back and forth between the canyon walls, then died away in the distance.

"Hold your fire!" called out Hugh. "It's Kinzie!"

Hugh waited a moment or two and then crawled up to the wall. He crawled quickly over it and dropped on the terrace floor. His breath came hot and thick in his throat. He rested his head on the paved terrace. Then he looked up into the dim face of Abel Clymer. The big officer was holding a carbine in his hands.

"Well, that was a fiasco," said Clymer.

Hugh sat up and nodded.

Someone moaned in the shadows. "Who's that?" asked Hugh.

Clymer spat over the wall. "Phillips. He caught a slug in his left thigh."

"Bad?"

"Thigh bone is broken."

Nettleton came to them. "You're all right, Kinzie?"

"Yes."

"Who would have thought that mad preacher would have done that?"

Hugh shrugged. "At that, maybe he's smarter than the rest of us."

"How so?"

"He trusted in a miracle. He got one."

"But they'll torture and kill him."

Hugh shook his head. "Mind-gone-far," he said.

"Meaning?" asked Clymer.

"They'll know he isn't right in his

mind . . . or is he? No matter. It's a profanation to kill such a one."

"But he'll die out in the mountains!" said Nettleton.

"Does it matter?"

Clymer looked towards the dwellings. Phillips groaned. "Now we've got another burden," he said sourly.

Nettleton touched his throat. "Why did Hastings attack them?" He shook his head. "It was madness."

Hugh nodded. "Matt never could stand this type of stuff."

"But he was so strong."

"The type that cracks suddenly. The *heshke* came over him—the wild killing craze. He's better off, like Morton."

Hugh got up. He walked to the tower and threw the snake into the lower room. Then he climbed to the water pan and bathed his face and raw hands. He went down to the small dusty room where Darrell Phillips now lay. Katy Corse had cut away the trousers and underdrawers from his left leg. Great beads of sweat dewed Phillips's white face. Now and then he gritted his teeth to keep from moaning.

Hugh knelt beside the wounded officer.

"The femur is broken," said Katy quietly.

Hugh glanced at her. There was little hope on her face. Hugh examined the leg. The slug was still embedded in it. "We'll have to get that slug out."

She nodded. "We have alcohol, knives, and I think there are some surgical implements in Nettleton's baggage."

"Get them. We'll need a fire in here to heat the water."

"Yes, Hugh."

He looked quickly at her. She smiled. "I knew you'd take charge," she said.

Hugh bathed Phillips's face after Katy had left. Phillips opened his eyes. "Where's Katy?" he asked.

"She'll be back."

Phillips closed his eyes. "I'm sorry I

panicked," he said. "It must have been hell up there on that cliff."

"It was."

He opened his eyes again. "How bad is it?"

"Bad enough. The bone is smashed, I think."

He beat a fist against the blanket. "Helpless," he said softly. "It was bad enough before; now it's sheer hell."

"They won't get you, Darrell."

The officer eyed Hugh. "You won't let them, will you, Kinzie?"

Hugh shook his head.

19

SWEAT soaked Hugh's clothing as he finished with Phillips. They had tried to soak him into insensibility with alcohol, but even so the young officer had groaned and writhed under the knife. Then he had fainted.

Hugh sat back against the wall watching Katy bandage the thigh. The fresh blood quickly stained through the fine cloth. Hugh fingered a ruffle which Katy had ripped from the last of Mrs. Nettleton's petticoats. Katy glanced at him. Hugh flushed and then stood up. "I'll get some food," he said.

"Never mind. I'll get it."

There were only six mouths to feed now. Hugh walked along the terrace. Clymer stood in the shadows with his carbine across his left arm. "How is he?"

"Are you really interested?"

"We're in bad enough shape without a cripple holding us back."

"There's a way out, Clymer."

"There is."

Hugh nodded. "Put a slug into his head."

Hugh walked away. Clymer gripped his carbine and raised it. Then he lowered it. "Not time yet," he murmured.

Hugh wiped the sweat from his face and began to cut the cooked meat into equal portions. He placed it on a tin plate and then kicked dirt and debris over the fire. He looked up at the mysterious walled-in fault above the fire. He wiped his knife on his filthy trousers, resisted the temptation to gnaw at a portion of meat, and then walked out on to the terrace.

Clymer eyed the plate. "Meat! Kinzie! I can't wait."

"We'll eat together."

They gathered in the room where Phillips lay. Hugh silently passed out the succulent meat.

"You're a miracle worker!" said

Nettleton. "By Heaven, Kinzie, this is delicious!"

They ate quickly. Clymer wiped his mouth with the back of his hand. "Any more?"

"No," said Hugh. He finished his meat.

Marion Nettleton picked at her portion, eyeing Hugh whenever she was sure her husband wasn't watching her. Katy judiciously fed Phillips the best parts of her portion and his. The sick man ate a little and then lay back covering his pale face with his right arm.

"What is it?" asked Nettleton. "By Heaven, the father-in-law would love this. I must get some for him."

Hugh stood up. "There's plenty available," he said. "I should have thought of it before."

Marion Nettleton stopped with her fork halfway to her mouth. "Hugh! What is it?"

"Never mind. Eat."

Clymer stood up. "Answer the lady," he said.

Hugh started for the door. Clymer gripped Hugh's shoulder and whirled him about. "Answer the lady," he said.

Hugh spat. "Listen, you big tub of guts: she's eating, isn't she? It's food, isn't it? Take it and be thankful."

Katy stood up and looked from one to the other of them. "I know what it is."

"Well?" demanded Marion.

"Rattlesnake," said Katy.

Marion Nettleton threw her plate across the room. She turned pale and suddenly jumped up and ran to the door, holding her hand over her mouth.

Clymer set his jaw. "Damn you, Kinzie!"

Hugh grinned. "The Lord will provide," he said. "Best damned diamondback steaks I ever ate."

Hugh walked outside. Marion Nettleton was bending over the terrace wall. Always the lady, thought Hugh. He walked to the tower and picked up the coiled picket lines. Then he walked around to the place where the fault had been walled in. His carbine leaned against it. He thumped the mortared rocks with his Sharps butt. It was as solid as Gibraltar, or so it seemed. He climbed up into the second floor of the tower and tried it again. He was rewarded with a hollow sound.

Hugh eyed the wall. A pick might break through, if he had one. A sledge might crack through, if he had one. He squatted at the window, studying the wall. Somewhere, in his past, he had once read a book on medieval siege operations. "Why not a battering ram?" he said aloud.

Hugh began to gather his materials. A heavy roof beam would do for the ram, but he needed a means of suspension. He went out on the terrace. Nettleton and Clymer were talking in low voices. They stopped as Hugh approached. Hugh explained his plan to them.

Nettleton rubbed his dirty face. "Do you think we can break through?"

Hugh shrugged. "We can try."

"If the Mimbrenos hear the noise they'll be suspicious."

"Do you have any other ideas about a way of escape?"

Nettleton shook his head. "Let's try it," he said.

It had taken them all of two hours to rig the device. Beams had been braced in the upper floor of the tower, and they had been extended through the window to rest against the wall. Hugh rigged plaited picket lines from the beams and from them they depended a solid beam, even with the second-floor window. There was hardly enough room to swing the beam in the little room, but they had no other choice.

Nettleton passed around a bottle after they finished. "Now what?" he asked.

Hugh took a good slug. "We'll have to figure out the best time to begin smashing the wall."

"We won't have much time once the Mimbrenos hear us," said Nettleton thoughtfully.

"Supposing we *don't* smash the wall?" asked Clymer.

"That's a damned silly question," said Hugh.

Nettleton took another drink. "I'll have the ladies ready," he said.

"What about Phillips?" asked Clymer.

Hugh stood up. "We'll worry about that when the time comes."

"I'm worried about it now," said Clymer.

"You mean you're worried about getting out of here yourself and to hell with everybody else."

Clymer reached for the bottle. "Some day . . ."

Darrell Phillips opened his eyes as Katy wiped his forehead with a damp cloth. "How are they doing?" he rasped.

"They've been up there for a couple of hours."

"We should have thought of that before . . . before this happened."

"We won't leave you, Darrell."

"I know you won't. But what about them?"

She patted his bristly cheek. "I'll stay with you," she said.

Marion Nettleton gathered her things together. Her stomach still rebelled at the thought of the horrible food she had partially eaten. She tied a scarf around her head and tucked in a loose strand of hair. Still, it had been Hugh Kinzie who had held them together thus far. Phillips would die. Maurice would bumble and fumble as he always had. Clymer, instead of paying his usual attention to Marion, had become preoccupied with something else. That left Hugh Kinzie. She sipped a little water to get rid of the taste of the meat. "And if he dies on the way," she said aloud, "so much the better!"

Maurice Nettleton, in his meticulous way, went about making sure everything was ready. Not that there was much to get ready, but it salved Nettleton's conscience. He knew he had lost command of the party even before they had been trapped in the canyon. Man after man had died or disappeared. It wouldn't be easy to explain, now that First Sergeant Hastings lay dead out in the canyon, for he had kept all the records. Nettleton shook his head. There would be a great deal of explaining to do. Still, they might look upon him as somewhat of a hero for getting the remainder of his party to safety. If only that loudmouth Abel Clymer had gone the way of the others.

Nettleton padded about. He gathered up the extra weapons and carried them to the tower. He filled the canteens and placed them with the weapons. He looked up at the ram and nodded in satisfaction. This would make a good story to tell in the officers' clubs when he got back to duty in the east.

He came out of the tower and heard a scrabbling noise farther up the triangular passageway. He walked east towards the noise. A big figure bulked in the darkness. It was Abel Clymer, down on his hands and knees, digging in debris. Nettleton opened his mouth and then closed it. Kinzie had accused Clymer of caching food for his own use. Nettleton stepped in between two buildings and raised the flap of his holster.

Clymer pulled something from the hole and dusted it off. He looked up the passageway and then felt in his pockets. He opened the saddlebag he had unearthed and lit a match. Swiftly he began to take something from the bag and stow it inside his shirt.

Nettleton walked forward. He drew and cocked his Colt. "Mr. Clymer," he said.

Clymer turned quickly. He held a fold of papers in his big hand. The match flickered out.

"What is that, Mr. Clymer?"

"Personal papers."

"You're sure?"

"Certainly!"

"Let me see."

"You have no right to see them."

Clymer extended the papers.

"Light a match, Mr. Clymer."

Abel Clymer produced and lit a match.

Nettleton looked at the papers. Then he looked up coldly at Clymer. "The government drafts from Fort Buchanan. How came you by them, sir?"

"I was protecting them, Captain."

"So? *I* am in command here. Give me the rest of them, sir!"

Clymer looked past Nettleton. There was no one else in sight. He slid a hand inside his shirt. Then he moved swiftly. He knocked Nettleton's hand up into the air. His right fist smashed fully against Nettleton's jaw. Nettleton staggered against the wall. Clymer snatched the Colt from Nettleton's weakened hand. Nettleton swayed towards Clymer. Clymer thrust out his big right hand and closed the massive fingers about Nettleton's soft throat. Nettleton struggled. Clymer forced the smaller man to his knees. Carefully he placed the cocked Colt on the debris. Then he closed his other hand about Nettleton's throat. There was no sound but the frenzied scraping of Nettleton's feet on the gritty earth and Clymer's harsh breathing.

Clymer lowered the lifeless man to the ground. He stowed away the drafts. Then he picked up the captain and carried him into a dwelling. He piled debris over the body. Then he stepped back and spat on the rude grave.

Hugh Kinzie looked at Marion Nettleton. "I just can't find him," he said.

"He must be somewhere around here."

"He isn't. I've looked high and low."

"Perhaps he went out into the canyon?"

"If he did, he'll stay there."

"Yes." She came close to Hugh. "There is a chance for us, isn't there?"

"Who knows? We can try. He looked down at her. "I'll look for him again."

"Do so," she said coldly.

Hugh walked outside. Clymer stood by the crumbling wall. "He isn't to be found," said Clymer. "Last I saw of him he was poking about on the slope at the west end."

Hugh eyed the big man. There was

something wrong somewhere. "We'd best get ready," he said.

Katy Corse was binding a splint about Darrell Phillips's smashed leg. The man was in agony, she knew, but she would see to it that he went along.

Darrell Phillips placed a hand on Katy's soft dark hair, vaguely wondering what it would be like freshly washed and combed with a ribbon in it. "A red ribbon," he said.

She looked down at him. "What was that?"

"Nothing." He raised his head. "Is there any hope, Katy?"

"We'll get you out."

"I mean, any hope for us together?"

She pressed him back on his blanket. "I'm sorry, Darrell."

He nodded his head. "I thought so."

She stood up. "I'll see how the others are," she said.

He waited until she left and then drew his Colt out from under the blanket. It was freshly loaded and capped. He cocked it and slid it under the blanket again . . .

It took time to get Darrell Phillips out of the room and on to the terrace. He stifled his groans, and mercifully fainted when Clymer bumped hard against his smashed thigh.

They placed him in the passageway below the water seep. Hugh wiped the sweat from his face. "We'll block the other passageways," he said, "so they can't break through."

Clymer nodded.

They piled debris in the triangular passageway to the east of the tower, piling it high and forming a rude abatis with shattered beams, six feet higher than a man's head.

Hugh checked everything. The two women stood in the passageway. Katy Corse held a carbine in her left hand. A gunbelt circled her slim waist. She tied the canteen straps together and placed the canteens inside the lowest room.

Marion Nettleton shook her head as

Katy extended a pistol to her. "I've never learned to use one," she said.

"It's simple. Cock the hammer so . . . point the muzzle and pull the trigger."

"I'm afraid."

Katy shrugged. She slid the extra pistol under her gunbelt.

Hugh looked at the three of them. "We'll wait until just before dawn."

"Why?" demanded Clymer.

"Two reasons. One, we'll have light to see. Second, we've got to give Nettleton every chance to get back."

"If he does."

Hugh looked at Marion Nettleton. She seemed unconcerned.

Hugh had gathered together a pile of sotol stalks. "We can use these for light in there," he said.

They all eyed each other. There was one thought uppermost in their minds: was it a dead end?

The hours dragged past. There was no sign of life from the Mimbrenos. They could afford to wait another day and then move in without trouble.

Hugh paced the terrace with his carbine in the crook of his arm. Now and again he looked up at the darkened roof of the huge cave, wondering about that mysterious walled fault. There was no sign of Maurice Nettleton . . .

The sky was lighter now. Hugh looked down into the canyon once more. He could see Matt Hastings' body lying there. "So long, amigo," he said quietly.

Hugh stopped beside Phillips. "We're about ready," he said. "I'll carry you into the lower room so that you won't get hit by debris . . . if there is any."

Phillips moved quickly, drawing his revolver out from under his shirt. "I'll stay here," he said.

"You're loco!"

Phillips shook his head. "No, I can't burden you. Get on with your work. Good luck."

Hugh moved a little.

Phillips raised the Colt. "No. Don't try. You've got Katy to think of."

Hugh stepped back. He passed the wounded man. "*Muy hombre*," he said.

Darrell Phillips smiled for the first time in many days.

Clymer eased his big shoulders through the opening into the second floor. He waited for Hugh. They placed their hands on the beam and tested it. "Ready?" asked Hugh.

Clymer nodded.

They swung together. The beam end thudded against the rocks and bounced heavily back. They swung again and again. "No good!" said Clymer.

"Keep trying, you big bastard!"

Sweat streamed from their bodies. The beam began a steady thud-thud-thud against the stubborn wall. The Hohokam had built well . . .

High on the northern wall of the canyon the Mimbrenos threw back their blankets as they heard the thudding noise coming from the Place of the Dead. They stood up and got their weapons . . .

A rock cracked and then fell from the

wall. Another shifted and then fell. The end of the beam was fraying and splintering. Again and again the tattoo went on. Sweat streamed from the bodies of the two big men and a foul miasma rose from their stinking clothing to mingle with the bitter smell of dust . . .

Silently the Mimbrenos came down the canyon wall, testing the dawn air with all their senses. They stopped on the canyon floor and faded into the unburned brush . . .

The beam smashed through. Clymer went off balance and hit the wall, Hugh hung on to the beam and grinned. "Made it," he said.

They smashed with renewed fury. Rocks and ancient mortar crumbled beneath the savage onslaught.

Darrell Phillips wet his lips and then began to crawl towards the terrace wall, inching his way along until he could pull himself up on his good leg. There was a movement on the slope just below him. A bushy head rose from the brush. The Colt roared. The big slug smashed the buck back down the slope.

Phillips set his jaw. The agony in his leg made him feel faint. He braced his elbow on the wall and fired at a darting Mimbreno. The warrior fell and rolled down the slope.

"*Zastee! Zastee! Zastee!* Kill! Kill! Kill!" chanted the aroused warriors.

Rifles flashed in the light of dawn. Bullets pattered against the dwelling walls and sang eerily off into space. Phillips fired twice more, adding another notch to his tally. Then he stood there and laughed.

The Mimbrenos had scuttled for cover, shrieking in dismay . . .

There was now a hole in the wall big enough for a man to get through. Clymer and Hugh worked swiftly, cursing in their mad haste. They shoved beams across into the hole. Marion was helped up the ladder by Katy.

They could hear the smash of rifle and pistol fire near the terrace. Clymer leaned out of the west window and snapped out a few shots from his Colt.

Hugh tightened his belt, thrust some sotol stalks into his shirt, then teetered across to the hole, carrying his carbine. He turned and looked back. Katy was standing there, helping Marion up on to the shaky makeshift bridge.

Hugh looked down into the hole. It was pitch black down there. He hastily lit a sotol stalk and waved it to make sure it would burn. He looked down again. The floor of the fault sloped steeply upward and was littered with something brownish. But he felt a blessed draught of cold air on his heated face. There was a way through!

He dropped the stalk. It was about ten feet down to the floor. Katy passed canteens and weapons across to Hugh. Hugh reached across for Marion. Her face was set as she came across. "Put your legs through and drop," said Hugh.

She shook her head.

"Go on, Hugh!" called Katy.

Rifle fire broke out again. Clymer fired

steadily. Hugh hung for a moment and then dropped, hitting hard on something which crackled below his feet, loosing a curious musty smell. He looked up, vaguely seeing Marion. "Drop!" he yelled. "Damn it, woman! Drop!"

Then she landed heavily beside him and clung to him. Above them they could hear the muffled roaring of guns. Katy landed beyond them. Then the big body of Clymer came through the hole. They clambered up the steep slope towards the fresher air, floundering through material which cracked and snapped beneath them. Hugh fell heavily. His free hand touched something smooth and round.

Clymer cursed. "Move on!" he yelled.

Darrell Phillips jerked as a slug smashed into his right shoulder. He shifted his Colt to his left hand and steadied the heavy weapon. Somehow he felt calm and cool. A bushy head appeared beyond the wall. Phillips fired, driving the buck from sight.

He raised his head. "Come on, you bastards," he said.

A knife flew through the air and struck him in the left side of the neck. He fired his last shot. Then a bullet struck him full in the forehead and he went down for eternity.

The firing had died away. Hugh struggled to his feet, still clutching the rounded object in his free hand.

"Light!" roared Clymer. He lit a match and held it out. They looked about them. Marion Nettleton looked at the rounded thing in Hugh's hand. Then she looked down at her legs, buried up to the knees in loose material. Then she screamed again and again as the match flared out in the draught.

Hugh dropped the brown skull he held in his hands. He moved, feeling the dry bones crackle beneath his feet. Katy Corse drew in a sharp breath.

Marion Nettleton screamed again and then became silent.

"Hell!" said Clymer. "It's their cata-combs!"

Hugh gripped Katy by the arm and pulled her up the slope. They could hear the others floundering around below them.

"You think they'll come through the hole?" called Clymer.

Hugh grunted. "Into here? You wouldn't get them within half a mile of this place if they knew it was here."

He cracked his head against a rock wall. He felt for a sotol stalk and lit it. The passageway was narrow, hardly wide enough for them to get through. He worked his way upward until he felt the coolness of the dawn wind pouring about him. Then suddenly his head emerged even with the mesa floor. "Wait!" he cautioned Katy.

He crawled out on the ground and lay still, listening and peering about. The brush swayed in the wind. There was no sign of life. He pulled Katy up beside him. She shivered in the coolness. "Thank God!" she said.

Clymer pushed Marion up ahead of him. Her face was pale and drawn. She dropped on the ground and lay still.

Hugh picked up his carbine. "I'll scout," he said.

He padded through the rustling brush. There wasn't a warrior in sight. He worked his way to the edge of the mesa and cautiously peered down into the canyon. There were no warriors down there either.

He returned to the others. "Keep your eyes peeled," he said to Clymer.

"Where are you going?"

"Down below."

"You loco?"

"You'll see."

Hugh slid down the slope, wrinkling his nose at the musty odour. He looked up at the hole. He could hear slurring voices faintly through the hole. He grinned as he thought of those superstitious bucks dropping down into the charnel house. He gathered up half a dozen skulls and threaded a picket line through the eye holes. Then he hauled them up to the mesa top.

"You damned fool!" said Clymer. He clamped a dirty hand over Marion's mouth to stifle the scream that trembled on her lips.

Hugh cut mesquite branches and bundled them together. He thrust one into a cranny and placed a skull atop it, facing the hole. "Just in case," he said. "Let's go!"

They walked towards the west, keeping to the lower ground. Hugh planted another skull at a place where they could make their way down the western slopes.

20

THE sun was high when they rested in a cleft which cracked through a great pillar of rock. There had been no sign of pursuit. Hugh let them rest for an hour, then drove them on. They descended the side of the huge brooding mesa and stopped again in the middle of the afternoon.

It was dusk when they reached a small stream. They filled canteens and then went on until the faint moon tinged the eastern sky.

Hugh looked back at the mesa. "Starvation Mesa," he said.

They reached the San Francisco in four days of hellish travel. In all that time Marion Nettleton spoke hardly a word. Katy took care of her as though she were a child, binding cloth about her small feet, and feeding her with the meat of a deer Hugh had killed. Abel Clymer didn't speak much either.

They rested at the river for two days, then trended north along its course, keeping away from the faint trails they saw. It was murderous going, but Hugh drove them like cattle.

They found a good spring after three more days of travel. Here they made camp and rested. Hugh killed another deer and fashioned rude moccasins for the women. It was as though they had wandered off the earth and were travelling on some unknown, uninhabited planet.

Hugh could feel the pebbles through the thin soles of his boots as he waded across the stream. He had caught a reflection of himself in a clear pool and hadn't recognized himself. His beard was matted and filthy and his clothing wasn't fit for a self-respecting scarecrow. He dropped on the far bank of the stream and drank the cold water. Then he left the stream and headed steadily through the rough mountains, heading for the Rio Grande. The others were three days' travel behind him, holed up in a cave near a good spring.

Suddenly he passed a huge outcropping of rock and looked out on a distant plain, mottled with the drifting shadows of clouds. There was a thread of dust rising not more than a mile away from him. The sun sparkled on something. He took out his field glasses with shaking hands and looked at the dust. "Troopers!" he said. "By God, Troopers!"

He led the two horses and mules up the rocky trail. "Hello the cave!" he called.

Abel Clymer appeared carrying his carbine. "Kinzie!"

Katy Corse came out of the cave and brushed back her hair with a tired hand. She smiled when she saw Hugh.

Hugh tethered the mounts and took a pack from one of them. "It isn't much as to quality," he said, "but there's plenty of it. I met a patrol from Fort Craig. They were looking for Apache raiders."

"Why didn't they come for us?" demanded Clymer.

Hugh looked at the big man. "I was

lucky enough to get horses and mules from them. As it was, some of them had to ride double."

"How far are we from the Rio?"

"About sixty-five miles."

Clymer was busy opening the pack. "We'll leave tomorrow."

"Yes."

Clymer ripped open the pack and reached for a chunk of jerky. Hugh clamped a hand on the officer's wrist. "Remember the ladies," he said quietly.

Hugh carried the pack into the cave. Marion Nettleton was lying down. She sat up at Katy's urging and obediently ate what was handed to her.

They ate silently, looking at each other. "I never thought we'd make it," said Katy.

"We're not out of here yet," said Hugh.

Marion Nettleton carefully brushed hard-tack crumbs from her filthy dress. "I'd like some cherries for dessert," she said.

Clymer stopped his sandwich halfway to his mouth. "What the hell!"

Marion smiled. "With fresh cream over them."

Katy stared at her.

Marion looked at Hugh. "I always have cherries when they're in season," she said. There was a peculiar look on her face. She touched her hair and then leaned back against the side of the cave. "After dinner I'll have them bring my pony cart around and we'll all go for a ride. I have two matched Shetland ponies."

"Hell," said Clymer. "She's gone looney!"

Katy looked at the two men. "Get out of here!"

They walked outside. Hugh reached inside his shirt and brought out a packet. He undid it and handed Clymer three cigars. He kept two for himself. "Lieutenant Espinosa sent these with his compliments."

Clymer bit off the end of one of the dry cigars and lit up. He eyed Hugh through the smoke. "You tell him what happened?"

"All I said was that we'd been attacked by Apaches and there were only four of us left. I didn't feel like going into details."

"Good."

Hugh looked quickly at the big man.

Clymer waved his cigar. "I mean, being as I'm in command now, I'll have to make out a report to the department commander, and I'll be blasted if I want to go through all the details."

"Yes." Hugh lit a cigar. "Funny damned thing about Nettleton vanishing at the last minute. You don't suppose he broke free by himself?"

"Hell no!" Clymer scratched himself. "You say we're about sixty-five miles from the Rio, eh?"

"Roughly."

"Hard trail?"

"Not too bad."

"How does it go?"

Hugh sucked at his cigar. "Past that big peak just to the north and east. Follow the San Augustin Plains north for a time, then head east again between the Gallinas Mountains and the San Mateos."

"That's all?"

"That's all."

"Seems damned easy."

"It is."

Clymer stood up. "Well, I'll clean up a little."

"There's soap in the pack."

Clymer nodded and walked away.

"I wonder if that sonofabitch ever thanks anybody for anything," said Hugh to an inquisitive jay bird.

The jay twitched his head and flew off. Hugh laughed.

Katy Corse came out of the cave. She looked down at Hugh. "Thanks," she said.

"It's all right, Katy. It's my job."

"We owe you our lives."

"Forget it."

She sat down beside him. "She's going back to her childhood, Hugh. She just told me she had more party dresses than any girl in town, and that she'd rule the

White House better than Dolly Madison when her father became president."

Hugh shook his head. "She'll be all right after a rest."

"I suppose the loss of Maurice did it."

He eyed her. "Marion? Don't be silly. She never thought of anyone but herself."

"She seemed to like you, Hugh."

He grinned, "*Everybody* likes me, Katy!"

She stood up and eyed the ruins of her dress. "I wish you could have brought us some clothes," she said.

"I'll go right back!" Hugh stood up. "I'm sure those cavalrymen will have at least four or five ladies' dresses in their saddlebags."

"You're a fool, Hugh Kinzie."

Suddenly he drew her close and kissed her hard. "I know," he said. "You'll forgive me, Katy? I did a lot of thinking when I was alone on the trail."

She returned his kiss. "There's nothing to forgive, Hugh."

They walked towards the cave. "Watch

Clymer," she said quietly. "He's been acting peculiar."

"He always did."

"He's been asking me if I was sure she'll live long enough to reach the Rio Grande."

"Very solicitous."

"He worries me."

Hugh shrugged. "You'll soon be rid of him," he said.

Hugh lay on his blanket listening to the voices of Marion and Katy coming from the cave. Katy sounded like a mother talking to a ten-year-old girl. The wind soughed through the trees. Clymer had rolled up in his blanket long ago and was asleep twenty feet from Hugh. Hugh lay there for a long time listening to the night sounds. Something was missing. Then he realized what it was. Clymer was a heavy breather and his deep breathing while he slept had always annoyed Hugh.

Hugh got up on an elbow and looked through the shadowy dimness towards

Clymer. Not a sound came from the big man.

One of the mules brayed suddenly from down in the hollow. Hugh stood up and picked up his Colt. He padded towards the hollow. Suddenly he stopped and looked towards Clymer. Best to wake him up if Apaches were prowling about.

Hugh stopped beside the big man and bent down to place a hand on his forehead in order to wake him up without startling him. He stared down at the sleeping man and then stood up. Quickly he stepped behind a tree. He eyed the darkness, listening for every sound. The soughing of the wind; the rustling of small rodents; the splashing of the creek.

Hugh circled around through the trees to his own blanket. Swiftly he gathered dry grass and placed it in a heap. He threw the blanket over it and patted it here and there to make it look as though a body were beneath it. Then he placed his hat at the head end. He pulled off his boots and placed them beside the dummy.

Then he eased into the brush and squatted there, ten feet from his bed.

Abel Clymer walked softly for a man his size. He had heard that damned mule bray but he had heard nothing from the camp. He eased through the scrub trees until he could see Kinzie's body beneath a bush.

Clymer drew his knife and tested the edge on a broad thumb. He wet his thick lips and felt inside his shirt for the government drafts. The game was all but won. First get Kinzie and then Katy Corse. Marion Nettleton was out of her mind. The whole thing fitted together neatly.

He'd be the biggest damned hero in the Southwest. All he had to do was say Kinzie and the girl had been ambushed on the last leg of the journey to the Rio Grande. Kinzie had done his job. Katy was not to be reached by money or threats. Marion was mind-gone-far as Kinzie had said of Isaiah Morton. No one would listen to her ramblings, and even if she did regain her sanity, Clymer could always say she had imagined many of the things which had actually transpired.

Hugh heard Clymer before he saw him. He squatted lower to get the big man against the sky. Clymer stopped behind a tree. Then Hugh saw the upraised arm and the knife. "Clymer," he said harshly.

Clymer moved with instantaneous reaction. He whirled and lunged towards the sound of Hugh's voice. Hugh foolishly rose to meet the attack. He was driven aside as though by a charging grizzly. His Colt flew from his hand.

Clymer whirled and struck savagely at Hugh with the knife. The tip raked across Hugh's chest. Hugh grunted in pain. Clymer laughed. Hugh jumped behind a tree, feeling for the knife in the sheath at his back. It was gone. Bark flew from the tree as Clymer slashed viciously at Hugh.

Hugh jumped back. Clymer charged again. This time Hugh gripped Clymer's knife wrist with his right hand. He stepped aside, thrusting his right leg in front of Clymer. Clymer fell heavily over the leg.

Hugh felt about for a rock or a branch. Then he was forced to retreat as Clymer rolled to his feet, roared like a bear, and came on again. Hugh's foot slipped and he went down before the mad rush. His wind was nearly knocked out of him. Clymer slashed at Hugh's face. The blade sank into the dirt inches from his head.

Hugh kneed the big man in the groin. They rolled over and over down the slope. Clymer's head hit a tree. He shook it. Then he got up to meet a straight left which drove him back. Hugh followed through with a right hook. Clymer was staggered, but there was a tremendous vitality in his body.

Hugh stepped back. His foot hit something. It was his Colt. Clymer hurled a log and came at Hugh, weaving a pattern of cuts and slashes at the air. He mumbled to himself.

Hugh fired from the hip. Clymer staggered as the slug hit home. He shook his big head and came on again. Hugh fired two more times. The shots awoke the echoes. Birds scattered from the trees.

Clymer swayed in a cloud of powder smoke. He stared at Hugh with bulging eyes. "Damn it!" he said. "I'm not supposed to die like this. Not General Clymer!"

Hugh stared at the big man. Then Abel Clymer pitched forward on his face and lay still with the powder smoke rifting where he had fallen.

Hugh thrust his Colt under his belt. He walked to Clymer and rolled him over. The cold green eyes were already clouding.

Katy ran to Hugh. "What happened?"

"He tried to kill me."

Hugh felt for the big man's oxlike heart. Something crackled beneath the filthy shirt. Hugh unbuttoned it and felt inside. His fingers moved in an unpleasant stickiness. He drew out a thick fold of papers.

Hugh stood up. He lit a match and handed it to Katy. He looked at the papers. "Government drafts," he said. He wiped the blood from his fingers. "I've done my job," he said quietly.

"He would have been quite the hero to come into Santa Fe with two women, one of them Boss Bennett's daughter, and with twenty thousand dollars' worth of government drafts in his hands."

"*Two* women? You didn't think he'd take you there to talk, did you, Katy?"

She shivered. "Come stay with me in the cave, Hugh."

"With *her* there?" He shook his head. "You stay with me instead, Katy."

She looked up at him. "All right, Hugh."

Hugh helped her up the slope. They did not look back . . .

They drew rein on a rise and looked to the east. There was a darker green line against the light green and grey of the brush flats. Hugh turned to Katy. "The Rio Bravo," he said. "The Rio Grande!"

She leaned over and rested a hand on his.

"I have more party dresses than any other little girl in town," a calm voice said behind them.

"Yes, Marion," said Katy.

"You must call me Miss Bennett."

"Miss Bennett."

"That's better."

Hugh turned north rather than south. "There are garrisons all the way up the Rio," he said. "We can travel in style to Santa Fe."

"It's all over, isn't it, Hugh?"

He shrugged. "I've cleared my brother and brought back Marion Bennett."

"*Miss* Bennett," insisted the calm voice behind them.

"Miss Bennett," said Hugh.

"You'll get your commission now," said Katy.

"Probably."

"I'll wait for you, Hugh."

He smiled. "I know you will. But it will be a long wait."

She glanced at him. "As sweetheart or wife, Hugh?"

"Both," he said.

Hugh looked back at the distant mountains, hazy purple and mysterious. They had taken heavy toll from the thirteen souls who had dared to enter them.

Hugh looked at the calm, peaceful face of Marion Nettleton. She had paid the greatest price, and yet the most merciful one. He looked at capable Katy Corse and knew he had a fit mate for himself. He had a woman to love and a war to fight. That was enough for any man.

THE END

Books by Gordon D. Shirreffs
in the Linford Western Library:

THE VALIANT BUGLES
SHOWDOWN IN SONORA
SOUTHWEST DRIFTER
SHADOW VALLEY
TOP GUN
AMBUSH ON THE MESA

Other titles in the
Linford Western Library:

McALLISTER ON THE COMANCHE CROSSING
by Matt Chisholm

The Comanche, deadly warriors and the finest horsemen in the world, reckon McAllister owes them a life—and the trail is soaked with the blood of the men who had tried to outrun them before.

QUICK-TRIGGER COUNTRY
by Clem Colt

Turkey Red hooked up with Curly Bill Graham's outlaw crew and soon made a name for himself. But wholesale murder was out of Turk's line, so when range war flared he bucked the whole border gang alone . . .

PISTOL LAW
by Paul Evan Lehman

Lance Jones came back to Mustang for just one thing—Revenge! Revenge on the people who had him thrown in jail; on the crooked marshal; on the human vulture who had already taken over the town. Now it was Lance's turn . . .

FARGO: MASSACRE RIVER
by John Benteen

Fargo spurred his horse to the edge of the road. Its right hind hoof slipped perilously over the edge as he forced it around the wagon. Ahead he saw Jade Ching riding hard, bent low in her saddle. Fargo rammed home his spurs and drove his mount up to her. The ambushers up ahead had now blocked the road. Fargo's convoy was a jumble, a perfect target for the insurgents' weapons!

SUNDANCE:
DEATH IN THE LAVA
by John Benteen

The land echoed with the thundering hoofs of Modoc ponies. In minutes they swooped down and captured the wagon train and its cargo of gold. But now the halfbreed they called Sundance was going after it, and he swore nothing would stand in his way—not Indian savagery of the vicious gunfighters of the town named Hell.

FARGO: THE SHARPSHOOTERS
by John Benteen

The Canfield clan, thirty strong, were raising hell in Texas. One of them had shot a Texas Ranger, and the Rangers had to bring in the killer. The last thing they wanted though was a feud. Fargo, arrested for gunrunning, was promised he could go free if he would walk into the Canfield's lair and bring out the killer. And Fargo was tough enough to hold his own against the whole clan.

SUNDANCE: OVERKILL
by John Benteen

Sundance's reputation as a fighting man had spread from Canada to Mexico, from the Mississippi to the Pacific. There was no job too tough for the halfbreed to handle. So when a wealthy banker's daughter was kidnapped by the Cheyenne, he offered Sundance $10,000 to rescue the girl. Sundance became a moving target for both the U.S. Cavalry and his own blood brothers.

DAY OF THE COMANCHEROS
by Steven C. Lawrence

Their very name struck terror into men's hearts—the Comancheros, a savage army of cutthroats who swept across Texas, leaving behind a bloodstained trail of robbery and murder. When Tom Slattery stumbled on some of their slaughtered victims, he found only one survivor, young Anna Peterson. With a cavalry escort, he set out to bring the murderers to justice.

SUNDANCE: SILENT ENEMY
by John Benteen

Both the Indians and the U.S. Cavalry were being victimized. A lone crazed Cheyenne was on a personal war path against both sides and neither brigades of bluecoats nor tribes of braves could end his reign of terror. They needed to pit one man against one crazed Indian. That man was Sundance.

GUNS OF FURY
by Ernest Haycox

Dane Starr, alias Dan Smith, wanted to close the door on his past and hang up his guns, but people wouldn't let him. Good men wanted him to settle their scores for them. Bad men thought they were faster and itched to prove it. Starr had to keep killing just to stay alive.

FARGO: PANAMA GOLD
by John Benteen

A soldier of fortune named Cleve Buckner was recruiting an army of killers, gunmen and deserters from all over Central America. With foreign money behind him, Buckner was going to destroy the Panama Canal before it could be completed. Fargo's job was to stop Buckner—and to eliminate him once and for all!